Advance Praise for *Savaging the Dark*

"If there's a single author working in the horror genre who deserves wider notice, it might be Conlon, whose astonishing *A Matrix of Angels* (2011) is the most wrenching serial-killer novel of the past decade. This follow-up button-pusher would pair perfectly with Alissa Nutting's controversial *Tampa* (2013), if not for the opening scene: a terrified 11-year-old boy gagged and handcuffed to a bed while our narrator, sixth-grade English teacher Mona Straw, licks the dirt from his feet. From there, we backtrack to learn of Mona's evolving infatuation with student Connor Blue, a kid as average and unremarkable as his teacher. Connor soon graduates from extra study lessons to yard work to an overwhelming sexual relationship, with every step utterly believable as Mona cycles through giddy elation, mordant depression, and, most of all, tortured self-justifications of her actions: 'The top buttons are undone on the blouse but that's because I'm just casually hanging around the house, no other reason.' Conlon's prose is so sturdy that Mona's impaired viewpoint (for example, her concern that the power of their relationship is shifting to Connor) almost makes sense before it plunges them both into unavoidable disaster. Conlon writes with literary depth and commercial aplomb; his days of too-little recognition seem numbered."

— Daniel Kraus, *Booklist* (starred review)

CHRISTOPHER CONLON

savaging the dark

EVIL JESTER PRESS

Savaging the Dark
Copyright © 2014 by Christopher Conlon

Evil Jester Press
Ridge, NY

This is a work of fiction, and any resemblance to persons living or dead is purely coincidental.

Cover art by Gary McCluskey

First Edition: June 2014

ISBN: 978-0615936772

Printed in the United States and the United Kingdom

ALSO BY CHRISTOPHER CONLON

NOVELS
Lullaby for the Rain Girl
A Matrix of Angels
Midnight on Mourn Street

SHORT FICTION
When They Came Back: A Horror Story
(with photographs by Roberta Lannes-Sealey)
The Oblivion Room: Stories of Violation
Herding Ravens
Thundershowers at Dusk: Gothic Stories
Saying Secrets

POETRY
Starkweather Dreams
Mary Falls: Requiem for Mrs. Surratt
The Weeping Time
Gilbert and Garbo in Love

DRAMA
Midnight on Mourn Street: A Play in Two Acts

AS EDITOR
A Sea of Alone: Poems for Alfred Hitchcock
He Is Legend: An Anthology Celebrating Richard Matheson
Poe's Lighthouse
The Twilight Zone Scripts of Jerry Sohl
Filet of Sohl: The Classic Scripts and Stories of Jerry Sohl

Straight? What's straight? A line can be straight, or a street. But the heart of a human being?

— Blanche duBois

1

I am not I. This is not me. I haven't come to this place, this end, *this*. I'm in a dream—a fever dream, vision, hallucination. Or a film, insubstantial figures of shadow and light flickering before me. Unreal. It can't be real. *This is not my life.*

Connor's green eyes watch me. His arms are above him, wrists handcuffed to the bed. I've had to gag him: one of his white T-shirts rolled up like a rope and tied tightly around his head, between his jaws. It must be terribly uncomfortable. I want to run to him, set him free, stroke his hair, weep on his shoulder, say, *It's all right, baby, I'm here,* and have him put his arms around me as he used to, hold me, whisper into my ear, *I love you, Mona, I love you so much.* That's impossible now.

He wears nothing but a pair of old shorts. They're stained yellow. The color runs down the crotch of the shorts and onto the bed under him. The stain darkens the sheets, as if it were blood running out of him, not urine at all. Otherwise he's naked, his skinny, hairless white chest quickly rising and falling, his pale legs splayed before him.

The bottoms of his feet are dirty, I notice. I slip the pistol into my belt and move to the bathroom, grab one of the faded old motel washcloths there. I run it under the cold water faucet for a moment, wring it out, and come back to him.

"Sweetheart? Let me wash your feet. They're not clean."

I crouch down but with an intake of breath he pulls his legs back.

"Come on," I say. "Don't be shy. You're dirty."

He studies me, his eyes wide. Sweat glistens on his skin. I reach out a hand—slowly, gently, as you might to a wounded bird. Finally he allows me to take his left foot in my hand. It smells, I notice, but I don't mind, not really. I move the wet washcloth over the foot carefully, making no sudden moves. I don't wish to frighten him. I've never wished to frighten him. Not once in my entire life.

I finish cleaning his foot and study it closely—the smooth uncalloused heel, the cute little toes. *This little piggy went to market...* He seems to tense but I look at him tenderly, shake my head, try to let him know that I'm not going to hurt him. Instead I lean close to his toes and kiss them, one by one, on their soft undersides, the sides that meet all the disgusting undergrowths of the world. I run my tongue between the toes slowly, watching him watch me. I lick the graceful arch of his foot and the tender heel.

Finally I put the foot down and reach to the other. He allows me to, doesn't resist. I study the foot closely. A small blood streak on his heel. Black smears—dirt? oil?—along the arch. Bits of the motel's shag carpet clinging, even tiny jagged pieces of plant.

I can tell from watching his eyes that he doesn't trust me anymore, doesn't believe I'll do the right thing, doesn't perceive that everything I've done has been for *him*. I'd hoped that washing his foot for him would convince him but it hasn't, not yet. But then I realize. Anyone, his mother, a nurse, could hold his foot and wash it with a wet cloth. A stranger could do that! But a stranger would not, could not do what I decide to: taking the still dirty foot in my mouth I extend my tongue to it, lick it slowly, suck it, swallow the grime and the blood and the oil—yes, it's oil—and take them all inside me, take away everything that makes his life unclean and bring it into myself. Bits of carpet, bits of thistle and grass. He watches me, as he always does. He doesn't try to move. Once he flinches slightly and I remember that he can be ticklish. But this is no time for silly games. I keep on cleaning the foot with my tongue and lips until it's as clean as the other. Then I put it down gently. Surely he knows now. Knows that I love him, and how much, how dreadfully, how unendurably.

It occurs to me that it's been a very long time since I've seen Connor cry. He cried a lot, once. Now, no. I suspect he doesn't want to give me the satisfaction, doesn't wish to allow me to see him open and vulnerable. Connor is closed to me now. I know that. He doesn't need to tell me. Yet my life is nothing without him, this eleven-year-old soul-stealer, this heart-thief. *My life is absolutely nothing without him.*

I hear a car pulling up fast in the parking lot outside, tires on gravel, automobile doors slamming, voices. Through a slit in the curtain splinters of light play on the wall opposite us: red-blue, red-blue. There is no siren. I'd thought that there would be sirens. It's quiet, really. I can hear their crunching footsteps and the static sounds of their car radios. How like a movie scene this is, a scene from some '30s or '40s crime picture by Fritz Lang or Raoul Walsh. I wonder if Connor realizes it as well.

Will they knock on the door? And if they do, will it be gentle, a meek little tapping like a shy child might make? Will a soft voice say, *Excuse us, ma'am, we're very sorry to bother you, but would you mind terribly opening this door?* Or will it be like in the movies, all bluster and man-noise, the banging on the door like the sound of a cannon? *Open up, police!*

Or will they not knock at all? Is that why they're gathering out there so quietly? Waiting?

Connor hears them too. I can tell. I sidle up next to him on the bed, pull the pistol from my belt again. His eyes widen as I switch off the safety. I want to touch him, caress him, hold him. I want to love him forever. I want to rip him to shreds.

2

Memory. The exact moment I knew that I wanted to be a teacher. I'm in high school, walking home after classes one day, books held close to my underdeveloped chest. It's a cool autumn afternoon, breeze caressing the branches around me, maple leaves tumbling before me in the road. Though I'm wearing my favorite blue cardigan I'm aware that my checkered skirt is a bit light for the weather: my legs are cold. I walk quickly to try to warm up.

Across the street I habitually take to get home is a soccer field. I rarely take any notice of it, or of the middle-school games that are played there, but that afternoon something strikes me about those shouting pubescent voices and I stop for a moment to watch. It's a boys' game: eleven- and twelve-year-olds in blue uniforms and gold ones charging up and down the field, jumping, kicking, falling. They don't strike me as being particularly adept—there are missed kicks everywhere, balls flying the wrong way, boys skidding on the grass and landing on their bottoms. And yet they're clearly having a good time, and I find myself enjoying their energy, their happiness. Lithe young limbs, arms skinny or muscular, legs fish-pale but quick. And their faces: I can see in some of them the men they'll become, the growth, the expanding, the hardening of features that will happen. It makes me wistful, somehow. These beautiful boys seem perfect, as if they are in their exact historical and emotional moment, as if someone should figure out a way to hold them there, suspend time, keep the game going forever.

I don't know how long I stand there, but when the referee blows a whistle and the game ends it's like being pulled abruptly from a dream. Daily reality slides into me again and I shake my head, move on. I think one of the boys in gold has vaguely noticed me, this tall older girl (all of fifteen!) staring at them from across the field. He seems to watch me for a moment before he turns back to his coach and friends and laughter and Gatorade.

As I make my way home it seems to me that I could enjoy spending time with such children. Certainly not as their coach—I'm hopelessly maladroit at all sports—but perhaps as their teacher? I wonder what it would be like. I think about my own teachers: Mr. Arnold, Mr. Vale, Ms. Owen. It's hard to imagine being them, standing in front of a classroom each day, talking, handing out assignments, grading tests. Though I spend five days a week in their company they never seem entirely real, somehow. And yet I know I'm smart, maybe as smart as some of them. I remember being shocked the previous school year when I'd overheard a student asking our English teacher, Mrs. Rocca, what old black-and-white film had the line "I think this is the beginning of a beautiful friendship"—and she didn't know! I was so embarrassed for Mrs. Rocca that I didn't have the heart to step into the conversation and tell her it was from one of my all-time favorite movies, *Casablanca.* My fellow student, a girl named Mary Rainey, went away empty-handed.

I don't think about the boys on the soccer field again, not for many years. But from that afternoon I have it in my mind that I will be a teacher, that it's my fate. My destiny.

***

But I was still half a person then, not a whole person. Since the age of twelve I'd been half a person, as lost and as clumsy and as despondent as any half-person would be. There was no whole me, no *Mona Straw,* only a crude, partial simulacrum, a shattered shipwreck, a body torn asunder. Sometimes I would look in the mirror and literally imagine myself without one-half of my body, stand there naked after a bath and see myself balanced on one leg, with only a single arm and half a head—one eye, one ear, a half-mouth. At twelve, at thirteen I wanted it to be true. I wanted someone to slice me from the top of my skull right down through my face and chest and belly and twat, tear away the other half *which had no right to be there* and discard it on some fly-strewn rubbish pit. I am not Mona Straw, I would think. I am not the real Mona Straw. There is no Mona Straw anymore.

3

Was there a Connor Blue, then? Yes, there was. Yes, yes, yes, yes, yes, yes.

I knew Connor Blue for years before he showed up in my fourth period class—"knew" in the sense that I'd seen him on the playground while I was on duty, perhaps said good morning to him occasionally. Once I broke up a fight that was threatening to begin between him and another, much bigger boy. Connor had gone to the Cutts School since first grade. There was nothing especially notable about him then: just another little blonde boy, spirited, a bit silly. Back then I rarely saw him, since the very young children were kept separate from the older boys and girls—they had different recess times, different lunch hours, different ends-of-day. I thought no more about Connor Blue than I did about any other child five years too young for me to have in my classes, which is to say hardly at all.

Later I imagined—convinced myself—that I'd known from the beginning that he would be special to me. Lying with our hair together on a single pillow, staring up at the ceiling and feeling the slow fan waft air over our skins, he'd say,

"When did you first notice me, Mona?—really notice me?" and I'd say, "From the first, sweetheart. From the first moment I saw you."

It wasn't true, but he believed me. He always believed me, then.

At night, after Gracie was in bed and I was exhausted beyond reckoning, Bill would turn to me in the bed and begin touching me, first gently, then more insistently. Years before I'd welcomed such attentions, when we were younger and thinner and we had all the energy in the world for carnal fun. But after I went through having Gracie, my body softened and spread. (So did Bill's, and he was already twenty years my senior.) By the time I was thirty I'd begun to feel old, old and tired. I would look in the mirror the way I did when I was a girl, remembering the fantasy of having half my body hacked away, and wonder what had happened to that child. My hair, a lifeless silver-blonde, hung limply to my shoulders. There were charcoal-colored smears under my eyes. My shoulders slumped, my breasts sagged. Oh, not terribly. Not humiliatingly. The objective part of my mind recognized that I was fairly well-preserved for a thirty-year-old woman with a child. Men might even find me desirable, if moderately.

Some years previously, just before Gracie, I'd had a momentary affair with a teacher at the school: George Cooper. He was flabby, middle-aged—my husband was older than George but much better-looking, and in better shape. But George and I had gone to an educational conference together—not together, no, but we were there at the same time, the only two representatives from the Cutts School. Our rooms at the hotel weren't far apart. He was married, had kids.

It lasted all of two minutes, the actual thing, the *act*. Him grunting and slobbering, me just lying there and feeling him shoving at me, wondering what had possessed me to come to this pathetic man's room. I felt sick immediately afterward, rushed into my clothes, said nothing to him. He sat in the bed, the bed on which we'd just disgraced ourselves, and smiled, all soft hairy fish-belly nakedness, his dick wet-shining and flaccid in the hard hotel room light. I could smell that he'd farted. He laughed as if what we'd just done together had been the most fabulous and joyous thing that anyone had ever done in the world. *For God's sake, George,* I wanted to say, *put your clothes on, you're disgusting!* But no, he wanted to do it again, started tugging at himself and asking me to come back to the bed. Aghast, I ran from the room in horror, spent the night shivering in my own hotel bed with the sheets pulled up to my eyes while George tapped at my door for hours, or what felt like hours. *Mona, honey, Mona, come on, we already did it once, one more time won't matter, please open the door, Mona, baby, sweetheart, Mona.* I pictured him out there in the hall naked. He wasn't, of course, but that's how I pictured him, his clumpy flesh jiggling as he knocked, fart stink clouding around him, tears running down his puffy cheeks, dick in his hand oozing fluid in a sticky string down to the floor. After some time he gave up and I heard his melancholy padding back to his own room, the door closing.

We never spoke of it. A year later he had a massive coronary. It felled him like a tree.

For years after the initial passion had faded Bill and I were still companionable in bed. There was rarely much spark or excitement, but how much can there be after more than a decade, a child, after the weight of years began to pile up not

just on him, but on me as well? It was more a friendly and
mutually supportive act than anything genuinely passionate or
even, really, in a sense, sexual. But at some point I grew weary
of it, of the fuss, of the first touching and eventual realization
of what was to come, the tiresome slow build for him (slower
and slower as time passed), the even slower one for me, all the
preparation, the mounting, the jostling and stabbing, the final
mess. Perhaps he felt the same way. We never talked about it.
But over time those initial touchings became less frequent,
until we were something like roommates, warm and friendly to
each other but only occasionally intimate. We concentrated on
being parents. Most of our talk—really, *all* of it—was centered
around Gracie. She became our lives, our lives entire.

There had been times that I'd noticed the boys in my
classes. I'd noticed how cute they looked in their basketball or
softball uniforms, how funny they could be when they were
trying to impress me with their athletic prowess—for they *were*
trying to impress me. At the time the Cutts School had a
curious lack of attractive young female teachers. There were
young women, yes, but very plain ones. One or two struggled
with obesity issues. It dawned on me one day, looking at my
drab hair and face and body in the mirror, that to the eyes of
an eleven-year-old boy I might be considered pretty. I might
even be the prettiest teacher in the school. The thought was a
revelation to me after years of desultory sex with Bill, after the
disaster of George Cooper. I never felt desired, but I suddenly
realized that I was, at least to young, uncritical eyes. I realized
it in the looks of the eyes of many of my boys, the boys in my
classes: half adoration, half something else, something that
maybe even they, at their age, couldn't define.

But I wasn't attracted to them. Not in that way. I was a perfectly conventional woman with perfectly conventional thoughts and values. I'd had the usual boyfriends growing up, the usual overprotective father, the usual concerned mother. This was in the '70s and '80s, decades for which I've never felt the slightest nostalgia despite the drumbeat of movies and TV shows that have focused on that time ever since. Dad owned a little café, Mom was a housewife; we lived in a perfectly respectable row house in Northwest D.C., the Adams Morgan neighborhood. It was a good place to grow up, I guess, as safe and secure as life in any city could be in the years before the crack cocaine epidemic turned Washington into a shooting gallery. Until the catastrophe, at least, we lived average sorts of lives (except, of course, that by definition my brother and I could never be "average"). But even afterwards I was an excellent student, a responsible person, a good girl.

I loved reading, especially gloomy romances—*Jane Eyre* and *Rebecca* and the like. I loved old movies, especially murder stories with Bogart or Cagney or Robinson and anything with a good *femme fatale* like Barbara Stanwyck or Lana Turner. And Hitchcock, of course—always and forever Hitchcock and his icy blondes, Grace Kelly or Kim Novak, the kind of simmering woman I dreamed of being. I liked new movies, too, of course—I saw *Star Wars* five times when I was a girl—but for me there was something special in the older productions, watching people who in many cases had been dead for decades magically alive again, their flickering shadowy selves plotting evil deeds, shooting guns, punching each other, tossing wisecracks. It was a strange, appealing sort of immortality.

From grade school I knew that boys liked me well enough, that I passed whatever internal tests they had amongst themselves to judge females. I wasn't brilliantly popular by any means, but neither was I an outcast. Other girls liked me. Boys talked to me. I had my first date at fourteen, when I was a freshman in high school: another freshman, a tall skinny boy named Stan Stevens, got up the nerve to ask me to a school dance. We went. It was neither magical nor disastrous; Stan was nice, we danced, he shook my hand at the end of the evening and thanked me. We went out once or twice more, casual things, then drifted apart.

Both Mom and Dad drank too much, but whose parents didn't in those freewheeling days? Whenever I saw adults getting together there always seemed to be beer, whiskey, those bottled wine coolers that were so popular then—our own refrigerator was perpetually stuffed with them. Occasionally I'd steal one to share with one of my friends and the sky didn't fall. They seemed sweet and harmless. I was used to my parents' voices slurring in the evening, used to the softening of their glances and the fuzziness of their expressions. Neither was mean or abusive. They just seemed to *fade* in the evenings, softly, like twilight turning to night. I never felt traumatized by their behavior. I never felt anything about them, really. They were stick-figures in my life, useful for an allowance or permission to go on a date but otherwise not terribly relevant. I didn't think of them as alcoholics, though my mother drank wine coolers from early in the morning the way I used to drink Mountain Dews. I didn't consider their drinking in any serious way. I didn't think they might have been assuaging their pain. I had no idea they had any pain they needed to assuage. I thought that all the pain of the family was within me, myself (my half-self), that I carried it for them, silently, heroically. I carried it but I kept it sealed off, like nuclear waste buried deep within countless layers of lead or whatever they use for such a task. I didn't let it hurt me.

They died in an alcohol-fueled car accident shortly after the end of my high school career. I hardly noticed.

4

I met Bill Lindner in college. I was an English major, having been practical and deciding I needed a subject I could teach to young people—literature was much more marketable than movies, which were in some ways my bigger passion. My inheritance, not large, paid my way. Bill taught Political Science, a subject in which I had no interest, but I needed the course to help fulfill my general education requirements. This was at a little school in upstate New York run by aging hippies, who by then—the early '80s, Lennon's murder, Reagan's rise—were sour, disillusioned people with a kind of siege mentality, as if they thought themselves the last bastion of peace and freedom and liberality left in the land. Teachers tended to sit cross-legged on the floor with their students in a circle around them. In good weather classes happened outside in the woods. Everyone was on a first-name basis; teachers socialized with students, students attended parties at teachers' homes where they drank and smoked pot. Love affairs, though officially frowned upon between the learned and the learning, were frequent and generally the most open of secrets. I was two decades younger than Bill, a quiet kid who rarely made eye contact with anyone but a couple of trusted friends. I wore the kind of flipped-up hairstyle popularized by Mary Tyler Moore ten years earlier, badly outdated then. Plain sweaters, blue jeans. I was nothing that stood out in any way, but Bill took notice of me.

I found him frightening at first—he was a fierce, articulate lecturer, slim and good-looking in an intense sort of way, though by then his encroaching male pattern baldness made his long hippie hair look a bit as if it were sliding backwards off his head. His beard, long and unkempt, was beginning to go gray. He wore beads around his neck, tie-dyed T-shirts, jeans, Birkenstocks. He was glamorous, a kind of campus-level celebrity: a political radical in the '60s, he'd met Martin Luther King during the March on Washington, interviewed Malcolm X for his college newspaper ("What can white people do to help the black revolution?" my future husband asked him, to which the revolutionary replied, "Nothing"). He'd done sit-ins, passive protests, been clubbed by riot police at an anti-Vietnam rally outside the White House in '71. I was just a shy, mousy sophomore—and still a technical virgin, modestly experienced with boys and their various erotic predilections but never having gone quite *all the way*. Bill, on the other hand, had had all the experiences one would expect of someone like him, including numerous affairs with students. He'd even been married briefly. Yet, as different as we were, something clicked between us.

I didn't know what to make of sex at first. I knew vaguely about female orgasms (learned quite young not through personal experience but by glancing hastily through a friend's older sister's copy of *Everything You Always Wanted to Know*

About Sex But Were Afraid To Ask) yet for a long time the idea was only theoretical. I enjoyed the closeness with Bill, the caressing, the feeling of deep and profound *togetherness,* but the actual physical sensation was fairly limited. I wondered what it was that he felt, what made him sigh and moan and thrust faster and faster until he finished, sometimes quite violently, inside me. My discovery of my own physical resources wouldn't come for years.

I liked men. As a breed, as a type. I liked their physicality, their strength, their aggressiveness. Bill had those qualities in spades; I felt protected when I was with him. I could stay quiet and unnoticed, the only not-quite-adult in the room, when we were with his friends— other teachers mostly—and they were arguing about Reagan's policies and whether he was deliberately setting out to destroy the poor or if they were just collateral damage in his insane, unprecedented military build-up. No doubt those people thought of me as just another of Bill's groupies, but in my senior year he married me.

We traveled a little—our honeymoon was in London, plays at the Royal Shakespeare Company and concerts at Albert Hall—but mostly stayed home. Bill had a cabin that had belonged to his parents in the mountains of Pennsylvania, a rustic area surrounded by pine trees that we would visit sometimes over long weekends—the kind of place where in warm weather we could walk around in the woods wearing nothing but sandals. There was electricity in the cabin, and a modern bathroom, laundry facilities, but otherwise it was fairly primitive—no TV, no telephone, no air conditioning, the only source of warmth a fireplace in the main room. In winter we would sleep there, in front of the flames; no space heater could keep the bedroom from chilliness. It was a nice place that we often visited when we were first together. Not so much later.

Marriage made me less drab, gave me some level of confidence and a feeling of being connected with other people in a way I never had while sitting in the semi-darkened living room of the family home, Mom and Dad quietly getting sloshed with *Starsky and Hutch* or *Barney Miller* playing on the TV. Soon enough I graduated—"Mona Straw" it read on the diploma; I'd kept my name at Bill's strong feminist insistence—and eventually got a teaching certificate, just in time for Bill to cut his hair and beard and take a job with a left-wing lobbying firm in Washington. He wore a suit and tie to work, something it took me years to adjust to; the beads and Birkenstocks vanished, never to be seen again. "It's time to put away the hippie stuff," he would tell his old teacher friends when they visited. "That failed. We have to work for change from within the system, not outside it." His voice would hold an aching sadness in it when he said such things.

Since my parents' property in Adams Morgan had long been sold, we bought a house in Silver Spring, just north of the city, in a nice middle-class neighborhood of bungalows built in the 1920s. Big beech trees and black maples lined the streets and filled the nearby park with its playground and little ribbon of river. The streets were safe. I found a job teaching English at the Cutts School. Soon enough there was Gracie.

It was my life. There was nothing wrong with it. Nothing at all.

5

It happened slowly, but it seemed to happen quickly. One Tuesday after Labor Day Connor Blue appeared in my fourth period English class along with twenty or so other newly-minted sixth graders. I took no special notice. Why would I? There was nothing unusual about him. A bit shorter and slighter than most of the other boys, but a good-looking kid, fresh-faced, blonde hair a bit wild and prone to cowlicks, green eyes, a spattering of cinnamon freckles over his cheeks. Bright, quick to smile. Cute. At first he hung around a group of boys he'd been friends with the previous year, just average boys who ran around the playground at recess or played touch football on the grassy fields. But that didn't last long. Connor seemed to pull away from them in the first weeks of school, to no longer engage with them much during class, to keep to himself during recess and lunch. It was during a lunch period I had my first real conversation with him. He was sitting under a tree reading a paperback book, an unusual thing for a boy to do. Since being on duty during lunch can be quite dull for a teacher—little ever happens, one simply stands there watching—I walked up to him.

"Hi, Connor."

He looked up and grinned, one eye squinting shut. "Hi, Ms. Straw."

"Whatcha readin'?"

He held it up for me to see. An old paperback: *Alfred Hitchcock's Stories to Be Read with the Lights On*. I recognized it as being from the informal honor-system lending library in my classroom.

"Do you like spooky stories?" I asked.

"Sometimes," he shrugged, looking back at the book again. "I like Alfred Hitchcock."

"Really? I'm surprised you even know who he was."

"I've seen lots of his movies. *Lifeboat. Rear Window. The Birds. Psycho.*"

"Wow. I'm impressed," I said, sincerely. "Which is your favorite?"

He considered. "I think *Psycho.*"

I smiled. "That's mine too. Do your parents have them on video? Is that how you see them?"

"Nah. My dad doesn't care about old movies. I watch 'em on TV. Sometimes I go to the video rental store and get one. When I have money. I like Humphrey Bogart, too. He was cool."

"He sure was. Have you seen *High Sierra?*"

He shook his head. "I saw *The Big Sleep.*"

"Ooh, that's a great one."

We were silent for a moment. I looked across to the playing fields, watched Connor's former friends running around with a football. "You don't hang out with them anymore, huh?"

"Nah."

"Why not?"

Another shrug.

I crouched down near him. He fidgeted, as kids often do when the teacher is giving them individual attention. "So how do you like sixth grade so far?"

"It's okay, I guess. Pretty easy."

I smiled. "Is my class easy?"

He smiled, looked at me again. "Pretty."

"You're a good English student, Connor," I said truthfully.

"Well, you're a good English teacher," he said.

I stood again, a slight sensation of oddness coursing through me. Sixth-grade boys weren't in the habit of complimenting my teaching skills, or those of any other staff member. It felt strange to hear him say it.

"Well, thank you," I said, starting to move off again. "Enjoy your book."

"Thanks, Ms. Straw!"

That was the entire conversation. Other than calling on him when he raised his hand in class, other than the occasional *Good morning* or *How are you, Connor?* spoken in exactly the same way to him as to all my other students, it was the first time I'd ever talked to him, really talked to him personally. In those moments he became an individual, a *person*, as opposed to the others. Just as they no doubt found it difficult to imagine me outside the setting of the classroom—couldn't picture me shopping for groceries or helping Gracie into her pajamas or making love to my husband—I couldn't really imagine them, either. What did boys that age do when they weren't at school, when they were home alone in their rooms with their thoughts and dreams? What was it like for a boy to grow up in the 1990s?

What did a boy like Danny Morehouse, one of Connor's former pals, do at home? All I could picture was a young kid sprawled in front of a TV or playing a video game on his computer—cliché images, but maybe true.

I found myself wondering a little about Connor Blue, but he didn't preoccupy my thoughts overmuch—no more so than a number of other students that year who seemed a bit different, quiet or sullen or angry. It was the usual mix. I tried to help them as I could, but the truth is that teaching a group of twenty or twenty-five kids English once a day isn't a good environment for being especially helpful. It's all one can do to keep order, to remember what points to cover that day, to hand back yesterday's homework and give out today's, to try to come across as reasonably cheerful and engaging. There isn't a great deal of time for one-on-one counseling sessions or personalized discussions. And so a girl like Lauren Holloway, who almost never spoke or made eye contact? I could try to draw her out in stray moments, but for the most part, since she did her homework and didn't actively misbehave, she was on her own. A boy like Richard Broad, always talking out of turn, squirming, getting out of his seat? I could send him to the office occasionally, perhaps at parent-teacher conferences gently suggest that he be screened for attention-deficit disorder. And someone like Kylie McCloud, who the other girls made fun of, always in her own world—tiny Kylie, with her asthma inhaler and eyeglasses that would slip down her nose, that same nose she kept buried in some big fantasy novel every period, every day? What could I do for her? Not much. Teachers are surprisingly helpless, really.

But something about Connor held my attention, this quiet boy who read books and liked old movies and didn't engage with others yet who always seemed happy to see me, quick to break into a grin and say, "Hi, Ms. Straw!"

"Hi, Connor! Whatcha readin'?" It became my set greeting for him, whether or not he was actually holding a book just then. But he was always reading something, and he would always tell me about it: *The Adventures of Sherlock Holmes*, *Call of the Wild*, *Lost Horizon*. Of course he asked me for recommendations, and I directed him toward writers like Madeleine L'Engel and Ray Bradbury. Boys who truly love to read are, of course, delightful for an English teacher to have in her classroom, and Connor was, in that way, a delight. Again and again I would be surprised that he had read one of my recommendations so quickly and could then return to me for such an intelligent discussion about it. We spent a lot of time on Meg Murry and Calvin O'Keefe and on Bradbury's Martians. And, of course, on old movies. I was amazed at his knowledge. He was familiar with not only Hitchcock, but Frank Capra, Preston Sturges, the Marx Brothers, James Cagney. Sometimes he would sit in my classroom through lunch, since fourth period was just before. Often two or three kids would be there, usually girls who liked to read or who didn't feel like going outside. Sometimes it would be just Conner and me, alone. We didn't say much. I would eat my lunch at my desk, reading (or pretending to read) a book or magazine while Connor sat with another book from the class lending library.

"Aren't you hungry, Connor?" I would ask him. He never seemed to have a lunch.

He would shrug. "Not really."

"Want my apple?" I held it up for him to see.

He brightened, as he always did when I offered him anything: a book, attention. "Okay!"

And we would sit there, far apart—he habitually returned to his seat in the middle of the third row—quietly chewing, the teacher and her bright, unusual student, unaware (were we?) of the disaster that even then was rushing to meet us.

6

Connor's father comes to parent-teacher conferences that fall: I see him step sullenly into my classroom, a tall cadaverous man with a buzz cut and mustache who smells of cigarettes. He wears a rancher's coat over a white T-shirt and tattered blue jeans. I smile, greet him, ask him to sit down, though I dislike him instantly. His face is pale and pockmarked, set in a perpetual expression of anger. I can see from his wrinkle lines that this man rarely smiles, and he doesn't now. Instead he sits in the too-small chair and glares at me.

"How's he doin'?" he asks. He doesn't bother to say hello, how are you. Nothing.

I go into my usual recitation, glancing down now and then at my gradebook for reference. Excellent reading comprehension, very good writing skills, average class participation. It all sounds very normal, yet as I talk I find myself growing nervous at his eyes, which never leave me. He never seems to blink at all. The eyes are watery green, like Connor's only with all the vividness and clarity and beauty drained from them. Somehow as he stares at me, listening—or pretending to listen—I begin to feel that his eyes are accusing me of something, that this man thinks me *guilty*. Of what? I talk on and on, not letting silence fall between us even for a moment. A 100 on the most recent quiz, that's very good, but his paragraph practice from last week wasn't as strong as it could have been and I wish he would speak up a little more in class because he's a bright boy Mr. Blue and I think he has a lot to offer.

"Him?" At last he breaks eye contact, looks down at the floor. His voice is contemptuous. "What does he have to offer?"

I swallow. "He's bright, Mr. Blue, really. He's very smart."

"Connor's dumb as a post. Always has been. All he does is watch TV. You sure you've got the right boy, lady? I'm Connor Blue's dad."

I scowl, though I try not to. "He's very smart, Mr. Blue. At least in English."

"That's news to me. His grades are lousy. Except *your* class." As if in accusation he holds up his report card, which I've not seen. I hold out my hand in a "do you mind if I have a look?" gesture and he hands it over.

He's wrong, but not *that* wrong. His grades aren't lousy, but they aren't great. Other than my B+ the card is awash in C's and C-minuses, along with a D in Math. I'm surprised. Connor can do much better than this, I know.

"Well," I say, handing back the card to him, "he's young, Mr. Blue. And it's still pretty early in the school year. I'm sure he can get himself on track. He's got a sharp, creative mind. And these grades aren't too bad, really."

He looks at me, disgust evident in his eyes.

"Is there someone at home who can help him with his homework?"

"I'm at the restaurant until late most nights. It's the school's job to teach him, not mine."

I ignore that. "What do you do at the restaurant, Mr. Blue?"

"Tend bar."

I nod. "What about his mother?"

"She passed away. Cancer. When he was two."

"Oh. I'm sorry." I think for a moment. "Does he have any siblings?"

"Nope."

"Well...we may be able to set something up here at school, if you like. We do have a tutoring program."

"That going to cost me anything?"

I've *really* begun to dislike this man now. "No, Mr. Blue. Students from the high school come in after school to help. It doesn't cost anything. I'll see about getting Connor signed up, if you want."

"Long as it doesn't cost anything." He stands impatiently, glaring at me again. "I don't want no bill showing up later. I'm not wasting any more money on Connor. It's sink or swim for him, as far as I'm concerned."

"No bill will show up, Mr. Blue."

He nods, then turns quickly and marches out. My mood lightens immediately the moment Mr. Blue is out of my sight. *My God*, I think. *The poor kid.*

The next day at lunch, having tossed my daily apple to him, I say to Connor, "Your dad came to conferences last night."

"Oh, yeah?" He bites into the apple.

"He showed me your report card."

"He mad at me?"

"Well…disappointed."

"I don't know why," he says, kicking the floor under his desk. "Those are the best grades I've gotten in I don't know how long."

"Are they?"

"Mostly I get D's and F's."

"Wow. You only had one D this time. So that's a real improvement. Congratulations."

He shrugs. "I'm not very smart in school."

"You're carrying a B+ in *this* class, Connor."

"Yeah, I guess. English is easier."

"Connor, about your other classes—" my fingers fiddle with a paper clip—"since you're in here at lunch most of the time anyway, I could help you. If you want."

He looks up brightly. "Really?"

"Sure. I mean, except the weeks I'm on duty. But otherwise I can help you. You could stay after school too. I'm usually here anyway."

"Okay. Thanks."

I look at him. "So what subject are you having the most trouble in?"

"Math. Always math."

"Do you have your book with you?"

"Sure. In my backpack."

I gesture to the chair beside my desk. "Well, bring your book and your assignment over here and we'll get started."

7

And so Connor Blue becomes something of a special project of mine. He still doesn't take up that much of my mental space—I still worry about Lauren Holloway's silence, Richard Broad's rambunctiousness, Kylie McCloud's nose always buried in books; I still have a life outside school too, with Bill and with Gracie who has just started pre-school this year, all sweet little schoolgirl outfits and a lunchbox emblazoned with images of the *Teenage Mutant Ninja Turtles*. But when the final bell rings at 2:45 and the kids bolt from their chairs, busily gathering their sweaters and backpacks and rushing from the classroom, as often as not they leave only Connor and perhaps one or two girls there. It becomes a pleasant place to be, Ms. Straw's classroom in the after-hours. I'm able to have extended chats with the kids—not just Connor—and the unofficial tutoring I do seems to help them. It's a casual atmosphere, with other children or the occasional stray teacher wandering in and out. I feel good, productive, useful. It takes time but I'm able to manage around Gracie's school schedule—she too stays in an after-school program. I have enough time to pick her up at the end of the day, hit the supermarket and get home to make some reasonable sort of dinner. Only as the evening wears on does the tiredness begin to hit me, after I've struggled through Gracie's bath and story and bedtime and drop myself onto the sofa next to Bill to wind up the night watching TV. When we go to bed, as often as not he turns to me and makes the slow movements I know lead in only one direction. Mostly I don't mind, but slowly, over weeks and months, I find myself growing impatient with his attentions, make excuses more often than I used to. He says nothing, it's not an issue between us. Yet.

After school my small group of students has its little tutoring and socializing time, but at lunch it's generally just Connor and me. I'm aware of how this could potentially look to others at the school, so I'm always careful to leave the window blinds wide open, the door ajar. And I tell other teachers about it, about the fact that I tutor him during that period, so there can be no mystery, no sense of secrecy or of anything inappropriate. The fact is, I enjoy Connor's company. He's a strange boy, awkward in some ways—he's clumsy, seemingly undergoing a growth spurt that leaves him uncertain of the dimensions and responses of his own body—but really extremely bright, and in unusual ways. I sense an enormous amount of untapped potential in this boy who can rattle off knowing references to movies fifty years old. Sometimes we discuss current films he's seen reviewed in the paper or on *Siskel & Ebert* on TV, but generally he seems more interested in earlier times. I took several film courses in college, and have a large collection of videos and movie books at home. I'm able to direct him to films he might want to watch—one day he comes in raving about *White Heat* with James Cagney. His enthusiasm is infectious, making me want to seek out movies I've somehow missed or watch old favorites again. I loan him cassettes of *Bullets or Ballots, The Roaring Twenties, Notorious, Spellbound.* I loan him the simpler of my many film books, volumes filled mostly with pictures, focused on Hitchcock or Lang or film noir. I've never loaned my personal things to any student, ever—eleven-year-olds are not wise stewards of other people's property—but Connor is extremely responsible, always returning the items quickly and in excellent condition. But that matters less to me than the gratitude in his eyes— thanking me for the movies and books, yes, but I think more for my *trust,* something I know he gets little of at home.

I'm curious—concerned—about Connor's home life, but I know better than to ask. Girls will sometimes come to a teacher unprompted, unload on her all their woes about their mothers and fathers and brothers, but boys tend to be reticent. Watching him eating his daily apple, pouring over the pages of one of the movie books I've loaned him, I wonder about him and his father. I don't know where they live or how much money they have, though judging from Connor's worn and faded T-shirts and blue jeans I suspect it isn't a lot. Does he come home to an empty house? How much is his father there? Does he eat decently? Does his dad ever compliment him on anything, support him, praise him?

Poor kid.

***

It's around this time that the dreams begin again, dreams that plagued me in high school but which I haven't had in many years. I'm twelve, I'm on my old red Schwinn bicycle, the asphalt rushing past me under the wheels, I'm swooping downhill on a beautiful summer's day, the wind blowing back my hair. I come to the intersection, glance left and right, the roads are clear, I glide through squealing with delight and, glancing over my shoulder, call out, *Come on, try to catch me, come on!* and as I look the other bike sails into the intersection and the truck, an old blue pickup truck which I only later realize was pulling out of a driveway I hadn't noticed as I'd passed through seconds before, collides head-on with the boy on the bike, I actually see the collision, I watch as the rusted front grill of the truck plows into his left side and his body bends strangely, an angle no body is meant to bend, the bike crumples under him and he goes with it under the truck and I slam into something, later I understand it was the curb, I fly off my bike and my forehead slams into the base of a maple tree, and all this happens silently, just as it did in life, or seemed to. I imagine the truck's engine must have made some sound but I didn't hear it. I know the driver never had a chance to swerve or hit his brakes or honk his horn or anything, the damned kid just flew into the intersection so fast, unavoidable accident, no charges, at least the man lived in another town so I wouldn't have to see him and his hellish blue pickup day after day, in fact I never saw him again, maybe he left the area, maybe he died. The boy's body bends at that bizarre angle, molding itself to the shape of the truck's grill, the boy's body is suspended there for an instant before it follows the bike underneath the wheels, I hit the curb again and again, my body briefly airborne, my forehead smacking against the base of the tree, I turn back with my head bleeding and my palms scraped and my knees of my pants ripped through to see Michael and his bike strangely intertwined, as if they were one single mangled thing there in the middle of the road, Michael, I don't move, I don't run to his side, I don't scream for help, I just lay there on the ground with blood running into my eyes and I stare as the driver of the truck who has leapt from his vehicle comes running back to him, as other drivers pull over, as people wave off traffic, rush to the crumpled thing there in the middle of the road and for a long, long time no one notices me, no one realizes I'm there at all on the other side of the street with blood on my face and palms and knees, and then the sounds finally begin, car sounds, panicked voices, *Oh my God* and *Call an ambulance, Jesus* and *No no no no* and finally someone points toward me, I see the white finger raised accusingly at me, I see its judgment, I see my doom, and I hear a woman's voice crying out, *That's his sister, look, there's Michael's sister, that's his twin sister!*

8

I don't tell Bill about the dreams, but he knows that something is strange, *off*, knows it as he has to shake me again and again in the night.

"Honey? It's just a dream, honey, it's just a dream, wake up."

I wake into my life, whatever life I have. I'm sweating and panting. I look in the darkness at my husband who feels like an interloper now, someone who doesn't belong here between me and my dreams, my memories. Who is this man with his bald head and soft belly? I push him away, rush to the toilet, vomit.

***

By day I function well enough. Sunlight and interactions with people bring me back to reality, what people call reality. Talking to Bill about the upcoming day, not mentioning the nighttime episodes. Pleasant with each other. A friendly kiss as he heads out the door, this one-time revolutionary, now a domesticated family man with coffee on his breath. Getting Gracie ready for school, packing her lunch—cheese sandwich,

Oreos, carrot sticks, juice box. Getting her into the car and heading off to the pre-school. Dropping her off, then heading the ten blocks to the Cutts School and becoming for one more day *Ms. Straw* to groups of unruly middle-schoolers. Yet I like Ms. Straw, she's comfortable, an easy and familiar persona I can step into and hide in. The children can't imagine the nighttime Ms. Straw, don't even know she exists. The feel of the bike seat on my bottom, the handlebar grips in my hands, the smooth road rolling by beneath me.

***

As autumn slides into winter the entire neighborhood seems to grow darker. Not the simple, obvious dark of seasonal change. Some other kind of dark, a dark I can't define as I wrap a robe around myself in the morning and push my feet into my old slippers and pad out the front door to get the paper. It's six-thirty in the morning and I can see dawn brightening the sky beyond the maple trees all around but somehow the light only seems to reinforce, to intensify the darkness it mirrors: rolled newspaper in hand I look around myself, at the familiar houses silhouetted against the morning, and feel as if there is some horrible secret looming here, some awful black nightmarish truth waiting to lean close to me and snatch me up, reveal itself to me, rip me to shreds. As if the shadows of the houses and the trees will come alive. I stand there in the driveway with my hair askew and a useless rolled newspaper in my hand, eyes wide, perspiration rolling down my face, my breath shallow. For an instant I see it, I know it, the doom that's waiting, the darkness that's approaching, ready to swallow me whole.

***

Again and again when I feel this despair, this panic, I find myself thinking of Connor Blue. Most of my students are blurs to me when I'm not standing before them, looking directly at them: I can't remember their faces, not really. A smile maybe, a pretty set of eyes, but not the actual face, not the *person*. But as autumn drains into winter I notice Connor Blue appearing in my mind increasingly often, increasingly vividly. I can picture him quite well when he's not around, even disturbingly well. I can't remember ever having this feeling about a student, though it's not really a feeling, it's more a sensation. I simply don't forget him as I forget the others. I can be making a snack for Gracie at the kitchen counter or vacuuming the living room carpet or driving to the supermarket or brushing my teeth and suddenly he'll be there in my mind, as vivid as the kind of religious vision reported by the old prophets. The blonde, nearly white hair, the way it sticks up in back and falls down in front, covering his left eye so that he has to brush it back with his hand. His green eyes, their steady expectant gaze, the long black lashes over them. The cute little nose, oddly small for his face and flat. The little-boy freckles splashed over his pink cheeks. And the smile, maybe the smile most of all, his thin cherry lips, his front teeth very slightly protruding—he'll probably end up with braces in a year or two—but very white, very even, very, yes, pretty. That's the word for Connor Blue: *Pretty.* In a couple of years he won't be. No boy is. He'll get his growth spurt—right now Connor is barely five feet tall—and his features will begin to change, elongate, harden. His voice will start to creak and crack and suddenly one day it will be deeper, harsher, no longer a boy's, high and fluty and insubstantial, but a man's instead. The clarity of his youthful gaze will vanish to be replaced by a more reserved, knowing, suspicious look. The quick innocent smile will disappear into adolescent lassitude and cynicism. It's a tragedy, really. It makes me understand why centuries ago the Italians favored castrati in their operas: to hold a boy just there, to not let him be corrupted by time or experience. Yes. And yet that would fail too: only their voices would remain pure, after all. The rest of them would still become men, inexorably, irretrievably.

***

The winter shadows deepen until it's hardly light at all when I gather Gracie up to head to her pre-school in the mornings, hardly light at all by the time I finish with the after-school study group in the afternoons and go home. In fact it's almost full dark. I see little light during my waking hours. Just little rectangles of it now and then during class, when I have a moment to look out. The way the buildings are situated much of the light is blocked, leaving me with the sense that the darkness is encroaching on me—*into* me—all the time. I function well enough. I teach perfectly adequately. I laugh with my students, I make jokes, I play around. I go where I'm supposed to go during the day, pick up Gracie when I need to, shop for dinner, greet Bill cordially, I'm agreeable to whatever sexual activity he suggests before sleep, say nothing about how distasteful I've begun to find his big, hairy body, his stubbly cheeks, his eternal coffee breath. The darkness is growing, inside me and outside. Inside like a cancer, outside like a truck grill slamming into me over and over again. I need light, purity, clarity, anything but this blooming winter darkness that seems to stifle and choke me.

9

Through all of this is Connor Blue and his sunshine smile and his old movies and his appreciation for anything I do for him no matter how small.

It occurs to me more than once that I have developed an unhealthy preoccupation with this boy, but I can't think what to do except to try to forget it. I've been a model teacher for Connor these past months. I've helped him learn sentence structure and spelling. I've tutored him in his other subjects, especially math, where his grades are slowly improving. I've been a support system for Connor, a cheerleader, just as a good teacher should be. I have nothing to be embarrassed about or ashamed of regarding Connor Blue.

And yet I've begun to feel that I'm hiding something from people, that behind the smiling Mona Straw they know is a subterranean other, a strange girl-woman whose mind is filled with smoke and shadows and darkness. This alternate Mona, this private soul, begins to alarm me. She's not unfamiliar— I've known her since I was a child—but something about her is becoming increasingly insistent, as if she were literally inside my body struggling to get out, to burst through my belly or climb up through my throat and take over my life, my family, *me*. For some time I don't know what to do about it. I wake in the middle of the night from sweat-drenched dreams, I turn away from my husband, my body goes haywire with menstrual blood and diarrhea and vomit. I miss days of work due to illness, something Ms. Straw *never* does. Lying in bed the entire day, all alone—Bill gone, having taken Gracie to school himself—weird visions seem to play in my mind and along the walls of the bedroom as I fade in and out of wakefulness. I hear voices, male voices, some consoling, some accusing, none speaking words but rather just sounds, guttural dark man-sounds. Except Connor's voice, which comes clear and sharp: *You okay, Ms. Straw?*

Ms. Straw is not okay. Ms. Straw gets over her bout of what she has decided to call the flu and returns to her routines, to her existence as wife and mother and teacher, but something seems wrong now, some aspect of the perspective she has on life has inexplicably shifted, tilted, changed. When she talks to her husband or daughter it's as if she is a clever impostor, someone with Mona Straw's exact face and body and voice but somehow not *her*. Some kind of unreality seems to come between Mona Straw and what other people think of as the world. Even at school, during class, she has this odd sense of otherness, a notion that she isn't herself anymore, that something has happened.

I try to talk to another teacher about it, an older woman named Estelle Higgins. We've always had friendly relations and I think she might be willing to listen. But as I try to talk about it I see the expression on Estelle's pudgy face begin to alter. I'm unaware of what I've said to her, actually. I'd begun with

Estelle, I have such strange feelings lately, I'm not sure what's going on with me but then must have gone somewhere very different because she's scowling in a perplexed way, a confused way, she's murmuring about how she has to get to class and how she hopes I feel better. Was I raving? I don't know what I was doing. Someone else seems to have been doing it. I wonder if the other, darker Mona, the one hidden away inside me, has come out, has climbed up through my throat and pulled her way into my mouth and opened my jaws and slipped out into the world, my world.

I find myself thinking less and less of Bill or Gracie. One afternoon I forget to pick my daughter up at school and I've been home half an hour when the phone rings, *Ms. Straw, where are you? Is everything okay?* I curse myself, rush out the door, make it back to the pre-school quickly enough. No harm done. Anyone can forget something. But there are other things. One afternoon when I pick her up she's crying. What happened? When she'd opened her *Teenage Mutant Ninja Turtles* lunchbox at noon today she'd discovered only the detritus from yesterday in it, a sandwich wrapper, an empty plastic bag containing Oreo crumbs, a crumpled juice box leaking drops of orange all over everything. I've completely forgotten to pack a lunch for her, simply handed her the lunchbox as she'd brought it home yesterday. A trip to McDonald's assuages her, and things are all right again, aren't they? Aren't they *really?* As I sit there with my coffee in front of me watching Gracie consume her Happy Meal I suddenly realize that I'm crying. I have no idea why.

"Mommy, what's the matter?"

Something has gone wrong somewhere, something's frayed and snapped, something's broken but I don't know what. I'm as absent-minded with Bill as I am with Gracie. I don't remember to buy dinner, or if I buy it I lose myself watching TV and forget to cook it. Bill tries to be good-natured, sensing something amiss, trying to jostle me out of it: "C'mon, Mona, where are you? I know you're in there *somewhere.*" But I'm not sure that I am. I'm not sure what I know and what I don't know anymore. I know that I have trouble focusing at school, forget to grade assignments, leave the educational video at home that had been my lesson plan, neglect to make up the regular Friday quiz. My faculty room box overflows with unread catalogs, unopened circulars. But I never forget the books I promise Connor, or the old movies. I never forget that we have a lunch meeting each day.

None of this is really too bad—not yet. The efficient and high-functioning Mona Straw has become somewhat scatterbrained, that's all. Her behavior is well within the range of normality for any person. People forget things. It's true that she rarely forgot anything before, but she's under a lot of stress. Having a husband and four-year-old daughter while holding down a full-time teaching job isn't easy. Everyone understands that, everyone backs off, gives Ms. Straw, *Mona,* some slack. But Estelle rarely talks to me anymore, rarely makes eye contact.

The truth is that there are times I can hardly take my eyes off Connor Blue. I realize this about myself and try to make sure no one notices. There's no one to see other than a bunch of middle-schoolers anyway, but they *would* if I weren't careful. What would they think if they realized? They're too young to imagine anything like, "Ms. Straw is in love with Connor!" The other way around, yes, but not *that* way, not at their age. And most certainly I am not in love with Connor. But at the same time I have trouble not staring at him, at his clear green eyes, his freckles, his small but muscular arm and graceful fingers as he moves a yellow pencil across a sheet of white lined paper. Yet he's no different from any boy in my classes, any boy anywhere. I know that. Every period my room is filled with young boys with clear eyes and muscular arms and high young voices. Connor's no different from the rest, I tell myself. Growing up with no mother and a cold, unsympathetic father? Let him join half the human race. Connor's no different. *He is not.*

***

But I can't convince myself of it, not during those private lunchtime sessions when he sits munching his daily apple and I watch him while trying to make sure it's not obvious I'm watching him. I watch his Adam's apple rise and then drop again as he swallows. I watch his eyes move across the pages of the movie book on the desk in front of him. I watch his left leg vibrating up and down and the slight movement of his foot within his sneaker.

"I want to see *The Thirty-Nine Steps,*" he says, looking up at me brightly.

"That's a really old one," I say, careful to hold my voice steady. "Hitchcock made that in the 1930s."

"I know. I'd like to see all those early ones. The only one I've seen is *The Lady Vanishes.* They run that on TV."

"Did you like it?"

"It was funny. Sometimes I can barely get what they're saying, though. Like, the accent."

"The English accent?"

"Yeah."

"Are you saying that the English don't speak good English?"

"Yeah! The English don't speak good English!"

We both laugh. The sound he makes is very high, girlish. His face is luminous. Hardly aware of what I'm doing, I stand and move to his desk, sit down at the one next to him.

"See?" he says, pointing at a photo of Robert Donat and Madeleine Carroll. They are out on some studio-created moor, handcuffed together. "*The Thirty-Nine Steps.* Looks good."

"It *is* good," I say, leaning toward the book, toward him. "I saw it years ago." I rest my hand on the corner of his desk, studying the photo. I'm aware that our fingers—mine are much bigger and longer than his—are inches apart. I wonder if he's aware of it too. I look at the handcuffed couple in the photo, and a picture flashes in my mind of handcuffs around Connor's thin wrist with an unbreakable silver chain leading to another cuff around my own. The movie, I remember, raised all sorts of implicit questions about how a man and a woman who hardly know each other would behave when handcuffed together. How would they manage the toilet, or their sleeping arrangements? What possible modesty could they maintain? Such questions obviously delighted Hitchcock. I find my heart racing as I study the photo, our hands, Connor's face in profile.

On his forearm, I notice, is an oval bruise, not too big, but impossible not to see. "What happened here?" I ask, pointing at it, my finger moving very close to his skin.

"That?" He looks at it as if he's never seen it before. "I don't know. I think I bumped into a door."

His mustached, bartending father crosses my mind. I let it go.

"Have you seen *The Lady Vanishes?*" he asks, turning the page and breaking the odd spell. I slip my hand off his desk and onto my lap.

"Yes, I have. You're right, it's very funny." Ladies, vanishing—vanishing into what? In the movie, into thin air. Here, in this classroom? Into…the words *child abuse* erupt suddenly in my mind. A sense of panic stings me and I stand, knocking my chair back awkwardly. Connor looks up at me, his expression slightly puzzled. Looking down at his sweet sinless face, I mutter, "I—" but can't manage to continue what I was going to say, if I was going to say anything at all. Sweat suddenly pours from me. My fingers and feet tingle. I back away from Connor, from the vision of the handcuffs and the bed and the bathroom, back away slowly as if he were some wild animal primed to attack and I his hapless victim.

"Ms. Straw? Are you okay?"

We're in the same room together but we're not, not really. We're not in the same world. I walk carefully back to my desk, drop down in my chair, try to breathe. How ridiculous I must look to him, I think. How strange.

I swallow and will myself to speak my words evenly. "I'm fine, Connor. I'm glad you're enjoying the book." Then, unable to stop myself: "I'd love to watch one of those movies with you someday."

***

I hurl myself into my work, spending extra hours on lesson plans and highly detailed grading and reading up in the kinds of educational journals that are always around in the faculty room but which I never bother to look at. I clean out my faculty box, glancing cursorily at the endless educational catalogs and offers and invitations from groups with names like Kidsplay and Mid-Level Readers' Club and Youth Leadership for America before tossing them in the garbage. I focus on Lauren Holloway and Richard Broad and Kylie McCloud, I counsel them after school, I call home concernedly, I *care* as only the best teachers do. I focus on Gracie too, playing jacks and hopscotch with her, helping her make clothes for her dolls, watching cartoons with her, reading with her, fun-splashing her in the bathtub to make her laugh and squeal. She's a wonderful child, actually. Very smart, very neat, pretty, mild-tempered. A mother could hardly ask for more. And I focus on Bill, I ask him how his work day has gone, make him his favorite dinners, rent movies I know he'll like—recent special-effects blockbusters, he's bored by old classics—and initiate activities in bed we've not done in years, or sometimes ever. He's flattered by all the attention but clearly a bit mystified by it as well. "Is everything all right, Mona?" Of course, everything is fine, how could it not be, what could possibly be wrong?

But none of this activity pushes Connor Blue from my mind for more than a few minutes at a time. When I dress for school in the morning I find myself wondering, even as Bill kisses me goodbye, even as Gracie runs around, what Connor will think of this pink top, how many buttons I can get away with leaving undone, whether he likes me better in pants or skirt, if I can wear the black heels or if they're too close to fuck-me pumps and then I shake my head violently and clear my mind of all such thoughts, toss what I'd begun to put on to the closet floor and go with the simplest, plainest professional clothes I have: long-sleeved white blouse buttoned high, tan skirt reaching almost to my ankles, plain brown flats. The woman staring back at me in the mirror looks like exactly what she is: a schoolteacher. Neither attractive nor unattractive. One of the invisible people of the world.

At school I find myself sometimes growing short with Connor, deliberately not calling on him when he raises his hand in class, dismissing his answers brusquely when I do. I abruptly cancel some of our lunch hours, claiming I have meetings. I all but ignore him in the after-hours tutoring sessions with the other students. He begins to look at me in a hurt way, his eyes darkening, his face tense with unhappiness. Or so I imagine. It's possible he doesn't care at all. But I think he does. I think it when his hand is up enthusiastically in class and we make eye contact and I turn away and call on another student, watch him in the corner of my vision and see his perplexed expression. He cares. I know he does. I think I know.

But I can't keep it up, any more than I can keep up my new enhanced perfect-mother perfect-wife perfect-teacher routine. One by one my new resolutions to do better fall away. I return to passiveness regarding Lauren and Richard and Kylie. I stop spending so much time with Gracie. At night I turn away from Bill, plead headache, tiredness, cramps. I return to myself. But I'm not there, not anymore.

10

When winter comes it comes ferociously, an early December storm hurling down a foot and a half of snow with near-blizzard winds blowing it around into whiteout conditions. School closes for days. Bill still goes to work, so I'm left alone in the house with Gracie watching videocassettes of *Pocahontas* and *The Lion King* and *Babe,* each for what feels like the twentieth time. Our power flickers, goes black now and then, lurches on again. The cable TV turns to static. I'm overcome with a sense of dread, a sensation that I'm entering a darkness from which I'll never rise again. I play with Gracie, let her "help" me make cookies and dinner, but I find a strange lassitude in myself regarding her. It's as if she's someone else's child, not mine at all. I'm soaking in the bathtub one afternoon, sweat pouring from me, my skin red and tender, when there is some kind of explosion that seems to rock the house. Gracie runs in panicked, I wrap a towel around myself, hold her hand as we look out the front window and see that a huge snow-heavy branch from the neighbor's white oak tree has crashed down on my car, crumpling the hood, cracking the windshield. Immediately it feels like judgment, a judgment on me, a sentence carried out on the guilty. Or at least a warning. I stare at the snow falling for a long time, stare at my broken car. Finally Gracie pushes something soft and warm into my hand, saying, "Mommy? Your towel fell off, Mommy. You shouldn't be naked in the window."

The storm finally passes, school reopens, life resumes. The car gets fixed. But when I arrive in my classroom that first day back it feels as if something has changed in me, some inner lens has undergone a permanent and profound refocusing. I realize that I've been lonely over this past week of snow days. I've felt adrift, lost. And yet when I look at Connor Blue come into the room for fourth period, enthusing to one of the other boys about the fun he'd had sledding yesterday, I know I've found myself again. I watch him make his way to his desk, drop himself down. His hair is askew, his cheeks flushed. He's talking about going sledding with another boy, Douglas Peterson, a good development—he needs to socialize more with boys his age, I know. But then I realize that what they're talking about is checking out a couple of the school sleds and doing it during lunch period today. My heart seems to drop into my stomach. I've not seen Connor in over a week and he wants to go sledding with his new friend rather than spend the time in this room with me? Suddenly everything seems to go gray in my vision, I feel my knees buckle. But I don't faint. I shake my head, right myself, welcome the students—"Hi Lauren, Hi Richard, Hi Kylie, Hi Douglas, Hi Connor"—and ask them about their snow day adventures before beginning the lesson. Stories of snowmen, snowball fights. Connor raises his hand and talks about sledding down the big hill near his house, his eyes bright and excited in meeting mine. Does he know how this hurts me? Is that why he's doing it? I don't want to believe it of him. But part of me suspects.

At the end of the period, as he gathers up his things and confers with Douglas about getting sleds, I say coolly, "Connor, may I speak to you for a moment?"

He glances up, seemingly unconcerned. "Huh? Oh, sure, Ms. Straw." To Douglas: "I'll catch up with you. Get two, okay?" The boy leaves, they all leave. In a minute it's just Conner and me alone in the room. He walks up boldly to where I sit at my desk. "What's up, Ms. Straw?"

But I suddenly realize that I have no idea what I want to say to him.

"Are—are you and Douglas friends now?" I ask in a small voice. I seem to be having trouble breathing.

"Huh?"

"You. And Douglas. Are you friends?"

He cocks his head. "I dunno. I guess we are."

"That's—that's good." I stare at his white sweater, at his soft young hands. His blue jeans are faded and frayed. I should buy him new ones, I think, and instantly dismiss the notion, tell myself I didn't think that at all.

"I guess." He looks puzzled. "Did you want something, Ms. Straw?"

"No, I..." It occurs to me then. "Connor, would you like to make some money?"

"How?"

"Are you good at shoveling snow?"

"Pretty good. I shoveled the front walk at our house yesterday."

The thoughts suddenly tumble into place, onto after another, dominoes falling.

"We have a back path," I say, "that leads to our storage shed. My husband hasn't gotten around to shoveling it. Would you?"

"Well, sure, I guess. But I don't know where you live."

I tell him. I don't tell him that I've looked in the file at the main office, learned where he and his father reside. It's in a different housing tract, a poorer one, but not more than a mile from us and on a main bus route. We talk about price for a moment.

"And you could use our snow shovel," I say.

"Okay." He smiles. "When?"

"How about tomorrow?" I say. "Friday. Could you make it on Friday afternoon? Should I call your father about it?"

"Nah, he'll be at work anyway. He won't care."

"Four o'clock?"

"Sure. Okay. I'll be there." He looks distractedly toward the classroom window. "Can I go now?"

I smile and stand. "Of course, Connor. Thank you."

He grins and runs for the door, stopping to pull on his old brown coat before scampering out onto Cutts School's gentle hills, green in spring, smooth and white now. I walk to the window where I can see him and Douglas pulling red sleds up the steepest hill on the property, which isn't very steep, really. Still, they ascend the hill, mount their sleds, slide down. I can hear their little boy cheers as they drop. My body tingles. Sweat trickles down my neck. Looking down at my hands I realize that they're quivering. Yet I've done nothing wrong, I know. *I have done nothing wrong.* This is a perfectly pedestrian arrangement between a teacher and her student, and what I told him was absolutely true. There *is* a back path to our storage shed where we keep our firewood, among other things. Bill *has* failed to clear it yet. What's more, I know Connor has no money. The few dollars I'll pay him for this service will be a godsend to him, allowing him to buy any number of things. Comic books. French fries at McDonald's. Admission to a movie downtown. Perhaps the back path doesn't really need to be shoveled with any urgency—we have plenty of firewood in the house anyway—but this kind of make-work project just shows once again how caring I am as a teacher. He's a poor boy. I've found an excuse to let him earn some money. No one could possibly criticize, no one could *judge*.

He comes the next day, fresh-faced and on time, his cheeks bright apple-red in the cold. Gracie is playing with a picture puzzle on the floor. Bill is at work. I watch my young student walk briskly up our front walk in his brown coat and red wool hat, ring the doorbell.

"Is that the boy?" Gracie asks. I've told her he's coming.

"Yes, sweetheart, I think it is." I run my hands over my hair nervously, smooth my blouse, go to the door and open it.

"Hi, Ms. Straw!"

"Connor. You came."

"Sure! I like money."

I smile. "I'll bet you do." My fingers flutter around my face, my hair. "Come in, Connor. Meet my daughter, Gracie. Gracie, this is Connor. He's one of my students."

"'lo." She glances up, then back down at her puzzle. Gracie doesn't care for strangers.

"Hi, Gracie!" Connor steps quickly over to her and kneels down. "Hey, you like puzzles, huh?"

She shrugs. "Sorta."

Connor studies it for a moment, picks up a loose piece and points out where it belongs. He hands it to Gracie to put in, and she smiles a little. He stands again, faces me.

"Well," I say, "are you ready?"

"Sure!" He looks around. "You have a nice house, Ms. Straw."

"Thank you, Connor. Step into the living room here. That leads to the back."

We do. Connor's eyes look around admiringly at the big-screen TV and big collection of videocassettes on the shelves. "Wow, Ms. Straw, you must have a hundred movies here!" He tilts his head sideways to look at the titles.

"You're welcome to borrow any that you want, Connor."

"Yeah, but you know what?" He looks at me sadly. "Our VCR's busted."

"Oh, no. Can you get it fixed?"

He shrugs. "My dad keeps saying he'll get around to it. It hasn't worked in a week."

"I'm sorry, Connor." I look at him. "Listen, the job's in back here." We step onto the rear porch. "See the shed there? There's a walkway to it, but you can't really see it in the snow. It's just sort of an indentation. See?" I point.

"Yeah, I see." He notices the snow shovel leaning against the house and grabs it in his mitten-wrapped hands. "I'll have it done in no time!"

I smile. "This is a big help, Connor. Thank you."

"Sure!" He grins brightly under his red wool cap, takes the shovel and marches over to the start of the walkway. I watch his shoulders as he works. He's energetic, stronger than I might have thought. He's very tidy, making sure each portion of the walkway is completely cleared before moving onto the next. I realize I should stop staring at him and turn away, look at Gracie who has come into the living room and is watching him too.

I have a vision, a sudden image in my mind, Bill and I, Gracie, we're together in this house and we're happy and normal and there's a fire in the fireplace and a holiday movie on the TV and hot chocolate with marshmallows in mugs on the table and Connor, if he's there at all, Connor is simply a neighborhood boy, my student whom I've hired partly out of practicality, partly out of sympathy, he shovels the walk in my vision and comes in and I pay him his money and he thanks me and out he heads into the fading winter afternoon, happy as a lark at his newfound wealth, running off to join Douglas or some other boy and frolic in the snow exactly as any sweet trusting eleven-year-old boy should. Yes. For an instant this is vivid in my mind, as bright and detailed as any vision can possibly be. And as evanescent. As unreal.

11

The lunchtime sessions become movie-watching sessions. I have a VCR and TV combination unit permanently in my classroom, after all. Connor's father is seemingly in no hurry to repair the equipment at home. And so I suggest to him that he can watch movies here at the noon hour. "You'll have to break a movie into two parts, probably, the lunch period isn't long enough," I say. "But you're welcome to use the equipment here."

"Wow! Thanks, Ms. Straw!"

He does. And watching *Strangers on a Train*, *Foreign Correspondent*, *Key Largo*, *Public Enemy* proves to be even more enticing than sledding with Douglas Peterson. The snow melts rapidly enough, anyway, soon nothing more than gray and white splotches on the landscape. For a while I fear that Connor may suggest that Douglas or some other boy come watch the films too, but this doesn't happen. I wonder why not. Maybe Connor simply knows that other boys his age aren't interested in such old movies. On the other hand, perhaps he senses something special about this time we spend together. He knows I don't offer the classroom at lunchtime or the TV and VCR to anyone else. In truth, I'm not even there every day: occasionally I have to attend a meeting or conference with a parent. Once I have to rush to Gracie's school because she's throwing up. (Mild food poisoning: she ate a crayon.) Still, I allow Connor to watch his videos whether I'm there or not. I trust him. He sees that, appreciates it.

But I'm usually there, sitting at my desk, watching with one eye as James Cagney or George Raft or Humphrey Bogart goes through his ancient black and white motions. The rest of my attention is occupied with lunch, or with grading spelling quizzes and practice paragraphs. Of course the truth is that little of my attention is really focused on any of these things. Instead I watch Connor, his enraptured eyes aimed at the TV screen. Occasionally he'll blurt out some sound of enthusiasm ("Wow!") or ask me something ("What does 'cracking wise' mean, Ms. Straw?"), but mostly he's quiet, an ideal filmgoer, completely fascinated.

As with everything we do together, our movie-watching is perfectly appropriate. I sit nowhere near Connor. The lights are on. The door is open. Every now and then someone steps into the classroom: a stray child, perhaps, who'll watch the unspooling film for a minute or two, grow bored and leave.

At last it snows again.

It's not a major storm, just a few inches, but it closes school for the day. Bill, in a generous moment, offers to stay home and take Gracie out for lunch and a movie. "Stay here and get some sleep, Mom," he smiles.

"Bill, thank you. This is so nice of you."

He shrugs, getting into his coat. "We'll give you a few hours of peace."

I wave to them as Bill pulls the car out of the driveway.

Then I stare at the phone for a very long time. I know Connor's home number; I've called his father a couple of times, good-news calls about Connor's excellent performance in my class. Connor won't be there, I know. He'll be out sledding with Douglas Peterson. He'll be out running errands with his dad. I know he won't be there. I'll call and there will be no answer, or I'll get their machine, or his father will pick up and I'll tell him how well Connor is doing again and hang up.

My throat is dry. My hands quiver. It's as if I'm a child again, an adolescent just on the cusp of dating and wanting, desperately wanting to call some boy but frightened to pick up the phone.

I pick up the phone. As I punch in the numbers I feel my body relax because I'm completely certain he won't be there. This is nothing, I think. Just a call to his dad. After all, he just got a 100 on his last spelling quiz. That's good news, sharable news. The line rings once, twice. Exhaling, I wait for the answering machine, his father's gruff *We can't come to the phone, leave a message.* "Hello, Mr. Blue," I rehearse in my mind, "this is Mona Straw, Connor's English teacher, and I just wanted to say how well he did on…"

"Hello?"

It's Connor.

I stammer, wipe my mouth with my hand. My fingers run shakily through my hair. Somehow I choke out the words *snow, shovel, work, pay.*

"Sure, Ms. Straw. I'll come over."

"You...?" My breath is shallow, short. "Connor, won't you be out sledding or...?"

"Nah. There's not really enough snow for that. I'm not doing anything anyway. I can come right away."

And he does. It feels as if it takes him twenty centuries to arrive and yet it feels, as I see him hustling coldly up the walk in his big coat, that he has arrived much too soon, as if he must have hitched a ride on a lightning bolt to have arrived so quickly. I'm wearing my pink blouse and blue jeans. The top buttons are undone on the blouse but that's because I'm just casually hanging around at home, no other reason. The same reason I'm not wearing a bra. I'm just a teacher on a snow day, that's all, sluffing around the house.

I open the door before he even knocks. We look at each other. Finally he says, "Hi, Ms. Straw."

I realize I've forgotten to speak. "Hi, Connor," I say, gesturing him into the house.

"Back walk again?"

"Yes, yes, that would be...great. That would be great."

"All right!" He grins, marches through the hall and the living room and to the rear door. I watch him shoveling. It doesn't take him long, there isn't much snow. But when he comes back in he's panting.

"Sit down, Connor," I say. "Take off your coat. Rest a bit."

"Thanks," he says, handing me the coat and dropping to the sofa. He has on a red-and-white striped shirt underneath. "I hope my shoes aren't dirty." He lifts each of his legs so that I can see the soles of his tennis shoes.

"No, they're fine. Just a little wet. Don't worry about it."

"Okay." He smiles, still catching his breath.

I sit gingerly on the hassock in front of the sofa, facing him.

"Where's your daughter?" he asks.

"My husband took her to a kids' movie. Would you like some hot chocolate, Connor?"

"Well, sure. If you have some, Ms. Straw."

"Of course we do." I jump up quickly, move to the kitchen, put on the kettle, pour powder into cups. My hand slips and one packet bursts out onto the counter everywhere: a spray of brown dust. I wipe it up quickly, not wanting Conner to see, anyone to see. I wait for the water to boil. Like his arrival, it takes twenty centuries. Finally it does and I pour it into the cups holding myself very steady and take the cups into the living room. Connor is looking at the long line of videos on the shelf.

"You sure got a lot of movies, Ms. Straw." He takes the cup. "Thanks!"

"Would you like to watch one, Connor?"

He glances at the shelf. "Well, sure…If you don't mind."

"I don't mind. I'll watch it with you. It's a snow day. We don't have anything else to do, right?"

"Right!"

"Do you think you should call your dad to let him know where you are?"

"Nah. He's at work. He doesn't care."

"Oh." I look at him. "Well, what one do you want to watch?"

He chooses *Double Indemnity,* one of my all-time favorites. Fred MacMurray and Barbara Stanwyck, their illicit relationship, her husband's murder. He sits on our sofa engrossed in the film. I sit on the other chair. After twenty minutes or so we're finished with our cocoa and I rise to take the cups to the kitchen.

"Should I pause it, Ms. Straw?"

"No, I can hear it, Connor. And I've seen this movie lots of times." I smile and, to my astonishment, reach out my hand and tousle his hair. I'd not intended to do that. He hardly seems to notice, continues staring at the screen.

I move to the kitchen, wash the cups. I don't have to wash the cups. We have an automatic dishwasher. But I stand there at the sink carefully rinsing each cup with hot water, applying a bit of liquid detergent, scrubbing each cup inside and out for several minutes, rinsing again. I wonder what I'm doing. What I'm doing here, at this sink, what I'm doing with this boy in the living room, what I'm doing with my life. And yet I'm so excited I can hardly see. The cups blur before me, the countertop sways. I'm hot, flushed. My arms tingle. I'm wet between my legs. I can't get over how pretty he is, how young, and how he's in this house, alone with me.

I return to the living room. MacMurray and Stanwyck are at the train tracks, disposing of her husband's body. I sit down on the sofa this time, hardly aware of what I'm doing. I'm on the other end, not close to him. Everything is perfectly innocent, appropriate, *explicable*. If Bill and Gracie were to come in at this moment they would be a little surprised, but there's no mystery. After all, Gracie even knows this boy. He's just finished shoveling our back walk. He's tired, he's sweating. I offered him cocoa and he wanted to watch *Double Indemnity*. I haven't even been here the whole time, Connor can attest to that. I disappeared for at least twenty minutes, washing those cups until they were as clean as they had ever been, as clean as anything could possibly be. It's all right. There's nothing wrong here.

The movie plays. After a while Connor says, "Ms. Straw, can I go to the bathroom?"

I smile. "Sure." I take the remote, pause the film, point. "It's up the hall on your left."

"Thanks!"

He gets up, moves quickly to the bathroom. The door closes. I don't listen, I try not to listen, but I can't help but hear, faintly, the sound of the lid being raised, the rustling of clothing, the liquid sound of his urinating. Then clothes again, flush, the sound of the faucet. Good boy, I think. He washes his hands.

He reappears, smiling, and drops down where he was on the sofa. As he sits I smile and take up the remote, simultaneously sliding closer to him. He doesn't seem to notice as the movie begins running again. I watch him instead of the screen, watch his bright eyes, his lips, the supple curve of his neck. I force myself to look at the film, a film which has never seemed so dull, so utterly irrelevant. As the movie nears its end I suddenly find that my hand is on Connor's hair, smoothing it, stroking it so gently that it's possible he hasn't even noticed.

When the film finishes he sits there unmoving, still staring at the screen which is now blank except for a bright blue glow. My hand hasn't left his hair. If he wasn't aware of it before, he is now. My fingers move outside my own control. I'm unable to stop them as they drop to his neck, gentle touches of the sort you'd offer to a small, frightened bird. The fingers move to his cute little ear, run softly around its edge. They move to his temple, his nose, across his lips.

"What are you doing?" he says finally, in a quiet little voice.

"Nothing," I say.

We sit there, my fingers moving over his hair and face for a long time.

"I have to go home," he says finally.

"Okay, Connor. If you want." I smile at him.

But he doesn't move. Neither does he look at me. He simply stares at the blue screen.

After several minutes he says again, "I have to go home."

"Okay." My fingers don't stop. They can't. I'm where I want to be, where I need to be, for the first time since I can remember. I want to be nowhere else, with no one else.

My hand finally moves down to his, covers it. I squeeze it gently, hold it. I turn it palm up and our fingers intermingle. He glances at our hands entwined, looks back up at the TV.

"I—" he starts to say. "I have...to go...home."

I think: You *are* home, Connor. But I don't say it. I lean to him, kiss him softly on his flushed cheek. He sucks in his breath. I can see the outlines of an erection pressing against his blue jeans.

Finally the sound of Bill's car pulling up in the driveway. I break away, drop his hand. I stand, listening as Gracie's voice comes over the sound of cars doors closing: "You shouldn't *do* that!" she shouts. She's laughing. So is Bill.

They crash into the house, all giggles and fun, as I'm pushing Connor into his coat. I introduce him to Bill, show Bill the good work he did out back. I pay the boy and lead him to the front door. "Bye, Connor!" I say loudly. "Thanks! Have a nice snow day!"

He stumbles down the walkway. He says nothing, looking back at me for a moment and then toward the street. He walks away very quickly, almost running.

After Gracie calms down she grows sleepy and I lay her down in her room. Then I go to Bill, and with no preamble at all kiss him deeply, press against him, pull him toward the bedroom.

12

Things are different between Connor and me after that. I can see it in his eyes. He'll stare at me for a long time in class and then suddenly look down, blushing. He still comes for movies at lunchtime but says little, rarely makes eye contact. When he does speak I can feel the effort he's making to sound as if everything is normal.

Of course everything *is* normal, I tell myself over and over. We've done nothing that couldn't be easily explained. Even the touching, the quick kiss—Ms. Straw felt sorry for her young student, that's all. She was being supportive, caring. After all, he doesn't have a mother. Yes, it's possible that for just a moment she got a little too friendly with the boy, in a way that wasn't wise, a way he might, in his innocence, misinterpret. A gentle reprimand might be called for: *Ms. Straw, we know how much you care about your students, and you're a wonderful teacher. But in the future be just a little more careful about the signals you may be inadvertently sending. Young boys are very impressionable.*

Connor lingers in my classroom now, more so than before. He seems reluctant to leave it at the end of lunch and at the end of the day. I can feel his eyes on me even when I'm not looking at him, even when I have Lauren Holloway or Richard Broad or Kylie McCloud with me at my desk, carefully going over their homework with them or trying to draw them out on how they're doing, how they're feeling. Ms. Straw the great teacher has reappeared, organized, professional, compassionate, caring, one of the stars of the staff of the Cutts School, liked and admired by students, teachers, administration, parents.

One day when Connor comes into the room and takes off his sweater I see that he has a big bruise on his left bicep, an ugly purple splotch. "Hey," I say casually, as the other students shuffle loudly in, "what happened to you?"

"This?" He looks at it as if he's never noticed it before. "Nothin'. Walked into a door."

This is the second time something like this has happened, with the same excuse. And the second time I don't believe him.

After class, as I'm putting the cassette of *Saboteur* into the machine, I say: "Hey, Connor?"

"Yeah?" He's drawing something on a piece of paper at his desk, doesn't glance up.

I sit next to him. "Hey," I say gently. "Can you look at me?"

He does.

"Is everything okay at home, Connor?"

"Sure it is," he says, scowling, returning to his sketching.

"Sure?"

He doesn't say anything, just moves the pencil on the paper. Circles, spiraling this way and that. We sit there for a moment.

"Can I come over again?" he asks finally, staring at the circles.

"Over?"

"To your house?"

I smile. "It hasn't snowed, Connor."

"I know. I can do other work. I'm pretty strong." He looks up again and, smiling, flexing his little bicep for me. "See?"

"I'm sure you are," I say. I look at him, at his crystalline green eyes, his pixie nose, the nasty bruise on his arm. "But..." Yet I can think of nothing to come after this word. I'm suddenly speechless. I look at him, aware of my breathing. Again the dominoes fall in my mind.

"We have a half-day on Friday," I say.

"Yeah."

"Maybe you could come then."

"Yeah, that'd be good." He smiles. "You'll pay me, right?"

I laugh. "Of course I'll pay you. I wouldn't ask you to work for free."

What I don't tell him is that Bill will be gone then, at a convention in Philadelphia, an overnight. And that while Gracie has an abbreviated schedule too as long as I call ahead I can have them hold onto her through the mid-afternoon.

"I'll have some projects for you to work on," I say casually. "And maybe when you're done we'll watch a movie. Sound good?"

"Sure!" His face is open, bright. I want to hug him then, this pretty boy with the bruised arm, tell him things will be all right. But of course I don't. I smile, get up and go to the VCR, turn on the movie.

The next two days I alternate between euphoria and low-grade panic. I cannot get Connor out of my mind no matter what I try. He's taken up residence and pushed virtually everything else out. I make my way through my classes well enough—I'm professional enough for that—but mentally I'm in another place. Gracie gets only a highly distracted mother, Bill a distant wife. I wonder if he'll start to think I'm crazy. Maybe I am, I think. But that doesn't stop the excitement, the beating heart, followed by the awful dread, the feeling of doom heading straight at me as unstoppably as a freight train. Yet I can't get off the tracks. Every time I try to move I only seem to get locked more tightly onto them.

I kiss Bill goodbye that morning, wish him a happy convention, see him off with his briefcase and overnight bag. I hustle Gracie into the car, drive her to pre-school, remind the teacher that I won't be back for her until three today. She assures me this is fine and that the after-school kids will have plenty of fun. "Yes, good," I say, or think that I say, jumping into the car again, driving too fast to Cutts, teaching my classes in a rushed and breathless way. Connor says nothing in class, seemingly just waiting, like the other kids, for the bell to ring and the half-day to begin. It does. He lingers after the others.

"See you at one, Connor," I smile. It's the time we've arranged.

He grins brightly. "Okay. 'Bye!"

The day has turned gray, cold, wet. Rain is slamming down by the time I get to my car, toss in my things, pull out of the parking lot and try to control myself, try to keep from pressing the gas pedal to the floor to get home. Or to get away, far away, any place except where I'm going. But my hands steer the wheel competently through the rain and soon enough I'm in the driveway, I'm home, I'm changing into a bright yellow blouse and short white skirt, I'm fixing my hair. My hands are covered in cold sweat. At any moment I expect to see Bill pull into the driveway, shaking his head in the self-effacing way he's developed over the years, since he grew staid and conventional, saying as I open the door: *You know what? I just realized I got the date wrong. The convention isn't until next week!* In a way I hope he does. I hope his familiar car pulls up behind mine in the driveway and I open the door and he comes in and we have coffee and he suggests we pick up Gracie and go for a drive or for lunch somewhere or dinner.

But he doesn't. Instead Connor comes walking along the street. He has no umbrella, no hat, just his big coat. He looks up through the heavy rain, double-checking that he's got the right house, and moves up the walkway. I force myself to wait until he rings the bell—not once, but twice. Then I walk to the hall and open the door.

"Connor! My gosh, you're soaked!"

"Yeah." He smiles, rain dripping from his nose. "Kinda wet."

"Why didn't you bring an umbrella?"

He laughs. "I don't have one!"

"Well, come in, come in," I say, clearing the way for him. "Take off your shoes, okay?" He does, leaves them near the door. "And give me your coat." He does. "Connor, this thing is soaked all the way through! You should have called. I could have picked you up or we just could have postponed or something."

He shrugs. "It's okay." But I can see that he's cold. Now that his coat is off I notice that he's shivering.

"Connor, it's not."

"I wanted to come," he says as I hang up his coat. "I need the money."

"Of course," I say.

"So what's the job? Is it outside?"

I look at him. "Connor, you're in no shape to work. You're too cold. Let me get you something hot to drink."

"I'm okay."

"Connor, you're going to drink something hot."

He shrugs again. "Okay. I wouldn't mind."

I seat him at the kitchen table. "Do you like hot tea?"

"Sure. Okay."

I microwave two cups of water, drops bags of mint tea into them, keep up some sort of line of chatter as I do so. I bring the hot tea and then go back for the sugar bowl. "I don't know how sweet you like it," I say. "Put in however much you want."

He puts in quite a lot. Finally he sips.

"Good?"

"Yeah." He smiles, still quivering. We don't talk for a minute or two. The house suddenly strikes me as extremely quiet, shockingly quiet. There is no sound but the rain and that seems far away.

Finally he says, "What's the job, Ms. Straw?"

"Connor," I say, my breath short, "you need to get out of those wet things. You'll catch cold."

He doesn't say anything. He doesn't look at me. After a moment he sips his tea again.

"I'm okay," he says at last.

"Don't be silly. You're shivering." I stand finally. "You can use our bathroom. I can give you a robe. We'll put your things in the dryer. They'll only take a few minutes."

He stands, slowly, looking down at the table.

"C'mon," I say, taking him by the hand. "Use this bathroom." I open the door for him, switch on the light. "Just take off your stuff and I'll get you a robe. We can't have you getting sick," I say brightly.

I close the door, stand there breathing fast. My stomach hurts suddenly. I feel as if I'm going to vomit. But it passes. I move off to the bedroom, grab a robe of mine for him to put on. He'll look silly in it but it's just for a few minutes, until his clothes are dry. I return to the bathroom. I stare at the doorknob. Has he locked it? If he has, I decide, I'll just knock gently, say, "Connor, I have your robe, just open the door a crack so I can pass it to you," and that will be that. He'll put it on, come out complaining that he looks stupid in this thing, we'll dry his clothes and I'll start him on his job. (What job? I haven't even thought.) He'll work, I'll give him a snack, the clothes will dry and he'll go back into the bathroom and lock the door behind him to put them on, he'll come out again, we'll watch a movie. All innocent, a comedy of errors, nothing important, just Ms. Straw hiring that Connor Blue kid to do some more work, that's all.

The door is unlocked.

I open it.

He's standing in the middle of the bathroom floor, facing away from me. He's taken off his pants, which are heaped next to him. His socks are gone, too. He's wearing his red-and-white striped shirt and a pair of white shorts.

"Here's your robe, Connor," I say, my voice oddly husky.

He doesn't move, just stands there with his hands at his sides as if he doesn't know what to do. I place the robe on the counter.

"C'mon," I say, moving to him. "Let's have your shirt too." I take it at its hem in both hands, as I do with Gracie's, pull it up as briskly and efficiently as a nurse would. I stand staring at his narrow white shoulders, the little freckles dotting it. He's so skinny. I drop the shirt, try to control my breathing.

"You're still shivering," I say quietly, touching his shoulders. "You should take a hot shower. Or do you take baths?"

"I don't take baths," he says, his voice small, strange. "I'm not a little kid."

I push my lips to his wet hair. He's shorter than I am; I have to lean down. "I know. I know you're not, Connor."

My hands, practically outside my conscious control, move to his shorts and slide them down. The shorts are at his feet now. I notice that they're not completely clean. For some reason this charms me, fills my heart. I stroke his shoulders, his back, his bottom, all of them covered in goose bumps.

"You *are* cold," I say.

He has virtually no hair on his body anywhere. What little he does have is sparse and so white against his white skin as to be nearly invisible. He has no pubic hair at all yet his erection is surprisingly big, like a man's. I reach around him slowly and touch it, stroke it gently.

"What are you doing?" he says, his voice shaking.

"Nothing," I whisper.

It takes only a few moments and he suddenly cries out as if in pain. His hips sway, his body shakes. He ejaculates wildly, spraying the floor and spattering the side of the bathtub. His knees buckle, he starts to collapse, I hold him closely, tightly. His legs quiver. His balance seems uncertain. I support him. We stand there together a long time as he regains his strength, his equilibrium.

Then, to my amazement, he begins to cry. His face contorts and big tears run down his cheeks and snot trickles from his nose. I turn him around then, press his face to me, kiss him, stroke his hair, say, "It's all right, Connor, shh, it's all right, sweetheart." It takes several minutes of gentle words and touching and reassurance for him to begin to calm. Finally I pull his head away from me and look at him, into his eyes. He glances back, looks away, sniffs, laughs a little.

"You okay?" I ask.

He nods, wiping his nose with the back of his hand.

"How do you feel?"

His voice shakes. "I never did that before."

"With a girl, you mean?"

"No. Like, ever."

I study him. "You've never masturbated, Connor?"

He shakes his head, looks away. "Some guys talk about it," he says. "They call it jacking off."

I laugh a little, gently. "Well, did you like it?"

He laughs too. "Yes."

"You should take a shower now, sweetheart," I say, smiling. "You're kinda messy."

"Okay." He glances shyly at me.

I let him go and he turns, stares at what's on the floor. I can see that he's astounded at what's come out of his body. He leans down and touches it with his fingers, studies it. Then he looks back up at me, grinning, blushing.

"Go on," I say, patting his bare bottom. "Get in. Don't worry, I'll clean up the mess. Do you know how the shower works?"

"Yeah," he says, stepping over the tub's edge.

I smile at this little naked boy and pull the shower curtain closed. After a moment he starts the water. I use toilet paper to clean things. Steam rises in the room. I step out for a moment to throw his things into the dryer, switch it on. When I come back I hear him turning the water off.

I pull a fresh fluffy towel from the drawer and open the shower curtain. "C'mere," I say. "Be careful." He steps out and into the waiting towel. I rub him. He giggles. "Am I tickling you?" I ask.

"A little."

"Well, let's see if I can tickle you a little more!" I goose him in his sides, run my fingers over his belly and thighs while he shrieks and tries to escape.

Finally we stop, breathless.

"Come in here," I say. Leaving the towel behind I take his hand and lead him into the guest bedroom. Smiling, I pull back the sheets on the double bed. "Sit."

He sits carefully at the edge of the bed. I drop down next to him. I lean him back, our heads touch the pillows. He blushes, giggles nervously. I kiss him, at first gently. After a while my tongue touches his and he draws back, eyes wide, a shocked expression on his face.

"It feels funny," he whispers.

"C'mere." I pull him to me. He doesn't move away again. I open my blouse with my free hand, lead his fingers to my breasts, my nipples. He stops kissing me to look down, to gaze at my body. His erection has already returned and he's tugging at it, making odd whimpering sounds. I take his hand, stop him, whisper into his ear, "Let me do it, Connor," and I do. This time when he comes he does it with more of a groan than a shriek. I carefully aim him away from me and he shoots it mostly onto the spare blanket at the foot of the bed.

He kneads at my breasts then, sucks my nipples, whimpers again, until finally his movements slow and stop. I realize that, cheek against my breast, lips on my nipple, he's fallen asleep.

I cuddle him for a time. My hands move between my legs, press, stroke for a while, not very long, and I come gently, gently but overwhelmingly, a huge wave cresting over me. I hold him, gasp, my hips quiver. But I don't wake him. He sleeps through it, like a baby. After a time I sleep too, sweetly, peacefully, my perfect darling boy in my arms.

***

Later I jostle him, push his shoulder gently. "Hey Connor, wake up," I whisper, kissing his temple.

It takes him a long time to come to consciousness. He's bleary-eyed, vague.

"C'mon, sweetheart," I say. "Up and at 'em."

He looks at me, then at himself. It's probably the first time he's ever awakened naked in his life. He nestles again my breasts. "I don't want to get up," he mumbles.

"You have to, baby. You have to put your clothes on. You need to go soon."

"I don't want to go."

I laugh a little. "I don't want you to go either. But you have to."

"Why?" His fingers toy with my nipple.

"Well, I have to pick up Gracie, for one thing."

He hugs me suddenly. His grip is strong, tight. I stroke his back, his bottom. Then, reluctantly, I start to pull gently away from him.

"C'mon, Connor," I say. "Time to start moving."

"I want to stay here forever."

"I'll bet you do. But you can't."

"Can we do it again?" Sure enough, his erection is starting to grow. He pulls my hand down to it.

"No." I pull back, take both his hands in my own, look seriously at him.

"Just *once* more?" he whines.

"Connor, come on. We need to get you dressed." He looks at me and his face grows petulant, but he moves away finally with a sleepy smile and reclines on the sheets. He stretches and then kicks his feet up into the air playfully. For a moment he looks exactly like a baby. It's all I can do to not leap atop him, kiss him deeply, let him do anything he wants to do with me. Instead I stand, all business now. "Your clothes should be done." I reach over, slap him on the hip. "I'll get them for you."

I walk out of the room and into another world, as any world is another world now when Connor isn't in it. The moment I'm away from him reality comes smashing into me.

My mouth goes pasty. I'm clumsy as I head to the dryer, bark my shin hard against the coffee table. If I can get him out of here, I think. If I can get him out of here and no one has seen us then it's all right. If I can wash the bed things and clean the bathroom then there will be no evidence. I'll have done nothing wrong because there'll be no evidence I've done anything at all. He could talk, of course. Connor could go to school and tell his friends all about me, about us. But Connor has no friends, I realize. He doesn't even talk to Douglas Peterson anymore. And his father? Would he tell Mr. Blue? Preposterous. I pull his clothes from the dryer, shake them out. He wouldn't tell his gruff, possibly abusive father a thing about this. Mr. Blue is the last one on earth he'd tell. And even if he did, the man would probably be proud. Connor's a boy, after all. It's not like it would be with a girl. Somebody would call me sexist for thinking that but it's true, it's *not* like it would be if it were some grown man with a little girl. No, it's all right. Everything is all right. There's nothing wrong.

I return to the guest bedroom and, grinning at him, toss the hot laundry onto his belly.

"Feels nice," he says, running his hands through it.

"Good?" I ask, sitting at the edge of his bed.

"Yeah."

"Go ahead, put 'em on."

He grins. "Make me."

"Connor, I'm serious." I note the clock on the wall: it's nearly time to go pick up Gracie. I can't believe how long we've been here together. It's felt like only seconds, sweet seconds. "You have to get dressed now."

"I never want to get dressed again. I want to be naked forever."

I laugh, shake my head, pick up one of his socks and toss it in his face. He throws it back at me and suddenly it's a laundry fight, his shirt and socks and shorts and pants flying between us as we shriek and giggle. Finally I grab his arms, pin them to his sides.

"Okay, mister," I say breathlessly, "now it really *is* time."

"Don't want to!"

"Oh, yeah?" I lean down and blow a huge raspberry on his belly. He laughs and kicks hysterically, tries to fight me, but I'm stronger and hold him fast.

After a while we settle again and I loosen my grip on his arms. He's splayed out on the bed panting, his clothes every which way across it. His erection is impossible not to see. I'm amazed at how resilient his young body is. Are all boys like this? I look at the clock again, realize I'm going to be late to pick up Gracie. But I can't leave him this way. I smile wryly at him, roll my eyes, shake my head, reach to him. In a minute or two he's finished again, breathing hard, semen splattered all over his legs and groin and stomach.

"Well," I say, using a Kleenex from a box on the bedside table to wipe my hand, "you wasted that shower you took, mister."

"I love you," he says.

That stops me cold. I look down at him for a long time. He meets my gaze, doesn't look away.

Finally he says it again: "I love you, Ms. Straw."

I laugh a little. "Sort of funny that you call me 'Ms. Straw.' Now."

"What should I call you? Your first name's Mona...right?"

"That's right."

"Mona. *Mo-na.*" He grins, shakes his head. "It sounds weird when I say it."

"Connor..." I hesitate. I pull more Kleenex from the box and start to clean him methodically. "Connor, you know that this is a secret, right? Us? This?"

"I know."

"You understand that it's very important you not tell anyone, right?"

"I know, Ms. Straw. *Mo-na.*"

"It's—it's really important, Connor. If anybody finds out we wouldn't be able to see each other again."

"I know. You don't have to tell me. I'm not stupid."

I smile. "No, you're not. But maybe...you know, you're hanging around with your friends, you start talking..."

"You'd get fired," he says, looking at me.

I return the look. He understands, all right. "Yes. I would." Arrested, too, almost certainly. As I look down at this sweet boy with his clear, innocent gaze—somehow even more innocent now, after what we've done together, not less—I realize suddenly how much power he now has over me. This eleven-year-old holds my life in his hands. But looking at Connor, at the adoration in his eyes, I know he'll never tell. He means it. He *does* love me.

I toss the tissues into the waste basket, knowing I'll retrieve them once he's gone and burn them or flush them down the toilet. No evidence, I think. No evidence and it's all right. No evidence and it never happened.

Our mood has gone serious. "Connor, honey, will you put your clothes on now, please?"

"Okay," he says. I watch him, watch his body vanish from me in stages until he's completely finished except for his coat and shoes. He stands beside me, taller than me now since I'm sitting on the edge of the bed. I touch him, put my arms around him, feel him embrace me. We hold each other, hold on for dear, dear life.

***

After he's gone I call Gracie's school, apologize profusely, say I got hung up in a meeting. The woman sounds considerably less patient than she had in the morning. "I'm sorry, I'm so sorry," I say, "I'll be there in a few minutes, just please give me a few minutes." I rush around the house, wipe down the tub and shower and tile floor, pull all the towels down—did he touch any towels? I can't remember—and throw them in laundry basket. Then I strip the guest bed, flush the Kleenexes down the toilet, push the blanket into the washing machine along with anything else that fits, switch the thing to *Hot*, the hottest water it has, the hottest water in the world, start it. I grab the half-filled tea cups off the table and run scalding water over them, soap them, rinse and dry them, put them back where they belong on the shelf. No evidence. No evidence and it didn't happen. *It did not happen.*

When I pick up Gracie I'm breathless, flustered. The woman tells me coolly that they'll have to charge extra for this after-hours care and would I *please* not repeat this as the staff has responsibilities of their own and the day is supposed to end at yes yes I'm terribly sorry it won't happen again I promise thank you thank you so much. By the time we get home the first washing is done and I pull the blanket and other things out, place them in the dryer, switch it on. Then I throw everything else into the machine and hit *Start* again. Gracie watches me, her expression curious. After a while she goes off to read her book in the living room.

Finally I close the door to the laundry room and things grow quiet. I sit in a chair near Gracie, close my eyes, breathe. It's done, I think. It's over. And it didn't happen. As far as the world is concerned it didn't happen. There's no evidence that anything happened.

A moment later Gracie looks up from her book and says, scowling, "That boy was here, wasn't he? I can smell him."

13

I am someone's mother.

I am someone's wife.

I am a teacher of young children.

I sleep alone that night, Bill away at his convention, Gracie tucked in bed in her own room. But I don't sleep. Not at all. I stare into the darkness. Shapes seem to form in it when I gaze at one spot long enough: circles, expanding vortexes about to engulf me. I thrash back and forth on the bed, pull the covers over myself, kick them off again. It didn't happen, I think. It didn't happen. That was not me. That was a movie, some grotesque child porn movie that somehow found its way into this house. I did not act that way. I did not do those things. My life is secure and complete with my husband and daughter and job. I have no need of anything else. I'm happy, satisfied. I have everything a woman could want. My marriage is a good one to a good man. My daughter is an angel. We have plenty of money. My job couldn't be more fulfilling. *I am a good person.*

I curl up in a fetal position, tremble violently in the dark. I push my face into the pillow, cry, cry for hours, cry until my head throbs and my muscles ache and my stomach hurts and the pillow is covered with tears and saliva and mucus. When I'm not crying I'm screaming, screaming with the pillow pushed tightly against my mouth until my throat is shredded and inflamed. Oh my dear God, I think. I'm a child molester. *I had sex with a child.* I can hardly swallow. I cough and blood spatters the pillow. I'm one of those people, those people you see on the news, teachers, coaches, priests, usually men but sometimes women. *Sexual predators.* That's not someone else anymore, it's me. That's my life. Back, I think. Turn backward, time in thy flight. Let me have the past twelve hours to do again. Or the past weeks, with Connor and I growing closer, ever closer, too close. I knew we were too close and yet I was unable to stop the train of catastrophe from racing at us, crushing us under its wheels. Let me do it again, those hours again, I plead with someone, anyone. I won't make the same mistake, I'll not invite him over at all, I'll not gaze hungrily at him when I know he's not looking, I'll not let my thoughts go wild and crazed, I will do everything differently *everything differently* please please I will.

Hours of this. All night. As a gray dawn begins to glow dimly in the windows I am utterly, comprehensively exhausted, flattened, dead. There's nothing left, I know. Connor will tell someone. Connor has been naked in front of Ms. Straw and she's taken his privates in her hands and made him shoot off everywhere and he's seen her breasts and nipples and held them and kissed them and he's kissed her on the lips and she's French-kissed him with her tongue and he will tell someone, he's bound to. He said his friends talk about *jacking off.* How can an eleven-year-old boy *not* talk? He'll talk. I know he'll talk. Bogart's line from *Casablanca*, absurdly, comes to me: *Maybe not today, maybe not tomorrow, but soon and for the rest of your life.* He might not talk today or tomorrow but he *will* talk and then for the rest of my life I'll be a criminal, a felon, jail time, damaged, dirty, sick, humiliated, unemployable, certainly divorced and never allowed to lay eyes on my daughter again let alone touch her or hold her. *Stupid!* I think, banging my fists against my head. *Stupid! Stupid! Stupid!*

And what if he doesn't? There are other ways it could come out. My body had been jolted, my face drained of its blood the moment Gracie had said, "That boy was here, wasn't he? I can smell him." Smell him! Of course. All his sweat, all his hormones raging. Of course my daughter could smell him. All the desperate work I'd done to wash the bed things and the bathroom and *dispose of the evidence* and it took a four-year-old girl only minutes to realize the truth. Not the whole truth. She could not even imagine the whole truth, at four. But enough to tell her dad, enough to make Bill wonder about his wife's preoccupation with this boy, why she would have him over when no one else was here, why she was so late (for he might find this out, too) to pick up Gracie that afternoon, why (maybe even this as well) she was suddenly in such a frenzy to do laundry, lots of laundry, unusual things like the blanket in the guest room. *What is going on, Mona? There's something you're not telling me.*

Yes, there is, Bill. Sit down and I'll tell you about what this boy and I do together when you're not home. I'll tell you what your ten years of loyal marriage to me have earned you. I'll tell you what being a good husband and father and always coming home at night and being caring and sensitive to us both has gotten you.

As the dull dawn slowly brightens I clench my eyes shut. It's gray and rainy and half-dark but it's too bright, much too bright for me to face. I can never face such light again. I don't deserve it. I can't stand it. But I'm too depleted to feel anything about it. All I know, all I realize, all I suddenly remember is that in the bottom drawer of the nightstand on Bill's side is a hand gun, an old pistol he insists on having around the house for protection. It was his grandfather's. I drag myself across the bed and reach to the drawer, open it. The gun is there, gray, ugly. I don't know what kind it is, I know nothing about guns. I've never shot a gun in my life, never held one until Bill brought this one into the house years ago and tried to get me to take shooting lessons. I would have nothing to do with it. I would only go so far as to hold the gun in my hands and pretend to aim it out into the back yard for a moment. After that I quickly handed it back to him. I'm terrified of guns. But now I need it. I take it in my hands. It's very heavy. I look at it. I don't know a thing about how it works, only where the trigger is. I hold the terrible gray pistol in my right hand and look down the barrel. I can't see anything, of course, but I look, hold my eye close, peer into it, study its particular darkness. Then I press the barrel to my right temple quickly and pull the trigger, or try to. But nothing happens. I look at the gun, realize that there is the lever in the back of it, above the handle, that you have to pull back for it to fire. I don't even know what the lever is called. The pulling back is called cocking, I know that. *Cocking.* They always do it in old Westerns when they're having a gun fight. I try to cock the pistol with my thumb, but I can't move it. I try to cock it with my other hand, but I still can't do it. My fingers are shaking, my heart smashing. I have to do this quickly or I'll never do it at all and I will live the life of a despised monster forever. I prop the gun between my knees and awkwardly pull with either hand until the lever finally snaps backward. The gun is now cocked, I know. The gun is cocked and all I have to do is aim and pull the trigger. I aim and pull the trigger. Again nothing happens. I look at the gun and remember that Bill told me about a safety switch, showed it to me. If the switch is on, the gun won't fire. I look, find it. It's on. I use my thumb to push it in the other direction, to *off*. I cock the gun, hold it to my head a third time, feel the hard barrel on my temple, clench my eyes shut, grit my teeth, and pull the trigger. The gun goes *snap* and jostles slightly in my hand but nothing happens. I cock it again, pull the trigger again. *Snap*. Again. *Snap, snap, snap, snap*.

The gun is not loaded.

I drop it into the drawer again, close it, fall back and lie motionlessly across the bed, this bed where once upon a time in another kind of life my husband and I conceived our beautiful daughter. I stare at the brightening ceiling. I'm beyond tears now. There's nothing left.

After a while I get up and start making Gracie's breakfast.

14

Yet in the light of a bright December morning, Christmas vacation upon us, the tree mounted in the corner of the living room with tinsel and decorations and lights, I can't think of Connor or what we did together in any way but happily, excitedly. I'm aware of the need for absolute stone secrecy, of course. I know what could happen. But that's the rest of the world, outsiders. They have nothing to do with Connor and me. They would never understand what's happened between us. Never. But it *has* happened. He's in love with me, we're in love with each other. It has nothing to do with molestation, with abuse. I did not molest Connor Blue. I loved him. I took a boy from a broken home whose father, I believe, beats him and I gave him pleasure, happiness, joy. I gave him the greatest experience of his life. I gave him something he'll never forget for all his days. I gave him love. And it was beautiful. It was not sick or perverted or any of those things the braying masses would call it. But I know they would never understand, know that this can never be spoken of, not ever.

At first I'd thought the holidays would have allowed us to see each other more but just the opposite is true. Without daily classes I don't see him at all. Day after day I live only my other, plebian life, the life of wife and mother and organizer of Christmas fun for Gracie, trips to the mall to see Santa and shopping for presents for Daddy and watching the carolers when they come to our neighborhood at night. I don't begrudge her any of this. I enjoy it, really. I want the holidays to be magical for her. For us, for all of us. We watch *A Charlie Brown Christmas* as a family, Gracie contentedly in my lap laughing at Snoopy's antics. We make Christmas cookies with green and red sprinkles. We watch *Santa Claus Conquers the Martians.* We watch *Miracle on 34th Street* and *It's a Wonderful Life* too, but sitting there with my daughter I'm overcome with yearning for Connor, wishing he were here with us to view these old classics. He'd probably think they're corny but how I wish he were here on the sofa with us to tell us that, holding my hand beside me while Gracie sits in my lap. How I wish I could adopt him, bring him here, keep him warm and safe with me always—not *instead* of Bill and Gracie, but in addition to them. To put the two parts of my life together without shame, without embarrassment. With joy. Bill would be a great dad to Connor. Connor would be a terrific big brother to Gracie. But I'm dreaming, of course. I know that. I know that in the real world Connor must remain a secret, must be treated as something dark and dirty in my life when he's not that, he's anything on earth but that.

Christmas goes by. On the way to and from the grocery store with Gracie I sometimes take a slight detour to pass by Connor's house, just to try to get a glimpse of him in his front yard or standing at the window. But I never do. Day passes day and I feel as if I'm going crazy waiting for him, waiting for this eternal damned holiday to end. It doesn't even snow, giving me an easy excuse to call him and ask him to come over. I know I must see him, see him soon, but there's no chance.

Yet finally there is. Bill's elderly mother has checked into a hospital in Boston and Bill decides to drive up to see her. Three days! He'll be gone three days! At first the thought was that we should all go, but we both know Gracie will tire the infirm old woman, make it impossible for Bill to have the quiet, peaceful visit with her he wants. It may be the final visit, after all. We talk of hiring someone to care for Gracie but three days is too long. In the end it obviously makes the most sense for Bill to go alone, for me to stay with Gracie for these few days between Christmas and New Year's. Yes.

The night before he goes he's feeling sexy and I'm so excited that I give myself over to him completely, in a way I haven't for a long time, swallowing my revulsion at his huge soft body, his hairy back, his bald head. It's all I can do to not be sick but I hold it in, hold it back, give him what he needs and smile and say love words to him. He's slow, awkward, loses his erection a couple of times. I'm patient, encouraging, though I can hardly tolerate him touching me, barely stand watching him pulling at his dick hidden in all that revolting pubic hair over his sagging scrotum and saying, "Just a minute, just a minute, I'll get it." I feel sorry for him, this aging domesticated revolutionary whose rabble-rousing days are so far back he hardly seems to remember them, or who he was then. But I do it because I'm so grateful to him, grateful for his giving Connor and me this chance, I would have exploded if I couldn't see him soon.

When Bill finishes—barely—he's panting with exhaustion and practically collapses on top of me. I want to scream, *Get off me, get off!* But what I do is whisper, "Thank you."

"What? Why?"

"Never mind. Just thank you."

Yet the usual child care is closed over the holidays, I discover, which leaves me in no better position than I was before. I nearly tear out my hair in frustration. This little girl, Gracie, this little girl! All I need is a few hours to myself. I'd take *one* hour. But Gracie is there, always there, tugging at my skirt, asking me to play with her, read to her, needing attention, needing to dress or be fed or take a bath. I call a few parents from her class and try to set up a play date for her with some other child, but people are out of town; the only parents who show interest are those who want to come to *our* house. No, no. I drop myself listlessly across the sofa, watching my darling little girl running around with a bunch of plastic flowers she found in an old drawer, strewing them across the room and shouting, "I love you all! I love you all!" like some pint-sized diva. She's adorable, I know, utterly, heartbreakingly adorable. But I have to get away from her, just for a little while. Yet I can't. A day passes and a night. I talk to Bill on the phone. He fills me in on his mother's condition, stable, I talk to her for a few minutes, offer encouragement, talk to Bill again, Gracie comes to the phone and says "Hi, Daddy" and asks when he'll be home, they talk, I take the phone back and tell my husband about his little diva with the flowers, laugh with him. When I finally hang up I push my fist to my mouth and order myself not to break down, not to cry.

When I put her to bed that evening I resolve to call him. I can't not call him. I must speak to Connor, at least hear his voice. What if his father picks up? I can't just hang up, they may have caller i.d., I don't know. I come up with a story—*Mr. Blue? Did I call you? Oh my gosh, I'm so sorry. This is Mona Straw, Connor's teacher. I was trying to call a friend of mine but looking in my little notebook here I accidentally dialed your number instead. I'm sorry. I hope you and Connor are having a nice holiday. Tell him I'll see him when we go back to school. I'm sorry to have bothered you.* Hang up. Good. I dial.

"Hello?" It's Connor, thank God, it's Connor.

"Are you alone, sweetheart?" I say quietly into the phone.

"Yeah. Dad's out. He won't be back until late. Sometimes he doesn't come back at all."

A pause.

"I miss you," he says finally.

"I miss you too, Connor, oh, you don't know how much!" I feel my throat tightening, tears starting to sting my eyes. "How was your Christmas?"

"It was okay."

"Did you get lots of nice presents?"

"Dad gave me twenty bucks."

I don't know how to respond to that. Finally I say, very quietly, "Do you think you could come over?"

"Is your family there?"

"Bill's out of town. Gracie's asleep for the night."

"Okay. If you think it's all right."

"It's all right. Be careful coming over. It's dark. Can you take a bus?"

"I'll just walk. It's okay."

"Don't knock. You'll wake up Gracie. I'll watch for you."

We hang up. I pace the room, sit down, get up again, pace again. I'm almost blind with anticipation, with *need*. Connor. Connor Connor Connor. But where? The guest room is right next to Gracie's, we can't go there. My mind flies around helplessly. The master bedroom? It doesn't feel right. But it's the only place. I want it to be *right*. I sit at the window, look out at the darkness, wait for his form to appear. It takes forever, but finally I see his big coat against the black night hustling toward the house. I go to the front door, open it as quietly as I can, breathe in the frigid air. When he sees me he runs, throws his arms around me, holds me tightly, breathlessly. I close the door, latching it.

"Shh." I hold my finger to his lips.

"I know," he whispers.

I pull his coat off, we stumble to the living room, fall onto the sofa kissing wildly, so hard that our teeth bang together and we pull back for a moment giggling. The room is dark, the only illumination coming from the twinkling little lights of the Christmas tree. Part of me listens for Gracie, for any sound of her stirring, but there isn't any. She's asleep, I'm sure. She rarely wakes up in the middle of the night anymore. I'm pulling at his clothes, he's pulling at mine, we roll onto the carpet by the tree, we're kissing and licking each other, his hips are bucking, he's rubbing his penis against my stomach, my nerves are berserk, I'm jamming his hand into my panties and between my legs and whispering frantically, *"Like this, like this,"* guiding him, pushing his fingers where they need to be, and in what seems like seconds a tidal wave slams into me, my back arches, I hear him groaning and feel warm liquid squirting onto my belly and breasts, we come together madly, deliriously, it never seems to end.

Finally our breathing slows. We lay on the carpet with sofa pillows under our heads. I laugh, tickle him lightly, kiss him.

"I love you, Ms. Straw," he whispers. "*Mo-na.*"

"Connor, I love you. You'll never know how much I love you."

We rest for a while in the twinkling darkness, the magic darkness. Our mood quiets. After some minutes he murmurs, "I never knew how a lady comes."

I laugh quietly. "Now you do."

"I mean, I knew that girls could. That women could. I just didn't know how it worked."

"You're an expert now."

"It was easier than I thought."

I look at him, laugh, stroke his jaw, run my fingers over his ears and through his hair. "You're a natural, sweetheart. You're great."

His grin is so big, so unreserved, so open, that I know he feels wonderful, strong, free, that he wishes to be nowhere else on earth but with me, here, now. We embrace, his semen sticky between us. I sit up, not wanting it to run onto the carpet. I need something to wipe it, so without preamble I slip off my panties and use them. I'm naked before him for the first time. It feels right, utterly natural.

"You're—you're *so beautiful,*" he says, reaching to my hip, stroking it, touching the hair between my legs.

"Surprised?" I say, smiling down at him. "At all this…stuff?"

"No. I've seen R-rated movies. I know how ladies look down there. But..." He stops talking, buries his face against me, pressing himself into my skin, me.

Finally I push him gently onto his back and straddle him, look down at his face in the Christmas lights. I play with him, coaxing his erection to return again, getting him ready. What I feel is so emotional, so deep, that if I try to tell him what I feel I'm afraid I might dissolve or explode. I can only deflect it with humor. I tilt my head to one side and whisper coquettishly, "Hey, big guy, you ready to lose your virginity?"

"I thought I already did."

I wink at him. "This'll make it official."

"I don't want you to get pregnant," he says.

That fills my heart. I smile, stroke his face. "I had an operation, sweetheart," I say quietly, truthfully. "After Gracie was born. I can't have any more babies. But thank you for saying that. You're very responsible, Connor. You're a real man."

Gazing at him I rise a little and then ease myself gently down onto him, feel him inside me for the first time.

"Good?" I ask.

His eyes are wide. "Oh my God." He laughs shakily. "Oh...my...*God.*"

I laugh. We move, sway, we swim on the wild waves for I don't know how long. We finish eventually, his eyes rolling up in his head, both of us joyfully arching together, becoming, for a moment, the same person in two bodies, one body, the same person in a third body which is simply us.

He catches his breath, calms, looks up at me.

"Okay...I'm officially not a virgin anymore, right?"

I smile, dangle my hair in his face. "You are definitely officially not a virgin anymore."

We touch each other gently, interweave our fingers, smile, giggle. Finally I climb off him, lay beside him utterly spent, perfectly happy. He rests his head in my arms. I'm covered in him, inside, outside. He caresses my breasts gently and slowly falls asleep. So do I, for a time. I've completely forgotten about Gracie, about anything. Nothing matters but the two of us here, now, forever.

***

Later he asks, "Why don't people in old movies have sex?"

"Well, they couldn't. Movies were censored back then. It wasn't allowed."

He moves his fingers, his tongue on me, in me. He giggles. "They skipped the best part," he says.

He leaves an hour before dawn.

***

I get a few hours' deep, dreamless sleep and feel more relaxed and happy than I have in ages when Gracie finally starts to get up. I've showered, made myself coffee and a bagel with cream cheese, gotten the paper and read it. The little kitchen TV is on to a cartoon, the volume low. I smile as she comes in wearing in her bunny pajamas and rubbing her eyes. "Hi, baby!" I say. "Have a good sleep?"

"I'm thirsty."

I pour some juice into a sippy cup and hand it to her, tousling her messy hair, leaning down and kissing her on the head. I pour her favorite cereal for her, add milk, put the bowl and spoon before her.

"When's Daddy coming back?" she asks, staring at the TV screen.

"Tomorrow, honey."

She nods.

"That boy was here again last night," she says finally, her eyes on the cartoon.

I swallow. "What?"

"That boy." She yawns.

I sip my coffee as naturally as I can. "What boy? What are you talking about, honey?"

"The boy who shovels the snow."

I try to laugh. "You must have had a dream, sweetheart."

"I didn't have a dream. I heard him. And you. Talking. You were trying to be quiet but I heard you."

I shake my head. "Just a dream, sweetheart. Nobody was here last night."

"I got up. You were in the living room with him. You weren't wearing any clothes."

I stand and move quickly to the sink, try desperately to not allow my breakfast to come back up through my throat. I splash cold water on my face. I'm suddenly shaking all over. This is madness, I think. It's all madness. This can't be happening. This is not my life, this is somebody else's life.

"He wasn't either," my daughter continues. "He looked funny. You were playing grown-up games." Her voice is oddly indifferent, as if this is a matter of no great importance.

I grit my teeth, swallow, *force* my coffee and bagel to stay down.

Eventually I turn to her, crouch before her. "Honey, can't you hear how weird that all sounds? Why would that boy come here in the middle of the night? Why would we take off our clothes in the living room?"

"You and Daddy take off your clothes."

"That's in the *bedroom,*" I say. "That's different. And we're married. Married people do that. Not other people. Honey, you just had a really vivid dream, that's all. I slept all night in Daddy's and my bed." I hold up my right hand. "I swear."

She looks at me, a curious expression on her face, then shrugs and turns her eyes toward the cartoon again. "I don't care."

I stand there looking at her, tousle her hair again, pretend to sip my coffee. Then all at once a terrible biting cramp clutches at me and I rush to the bathroom, drop down onto the toilet, let loose the worst explosion of diarrhea I've ever had in my life. I weep, emptying myself of everything in me, sitting in my own shit, weep uncontrollably, my face buried in my hands, my heart tearing to pieces, my soul splintering.

15

We don't see each other again during the holidays. We can't. I call him once, the next night, tell him that Gracie knows, that she heard us (I don't mention that she saw us), that we have to stop for a while. He says he doesn't want to stop, he wants to come over now, he misses me. He starts to cry. I know I'm failing him, he feels abandoned, discarded, lost. At the same moment Gracie moans from the bedroom, "Mommy?" I know the sound, she's had a bad dream. "Connor, I have to go, we'll see each other at school, we'll talk, I swear we'll talk, I have to go."

I hang up, sick with guilt, run to Gracie's room, hold her, tell her everything's all right. While I'm comforting her the phone rings. It rings four times and then stops. The machine is picking it up, I know. A minute later it rings again, four times. Then silence. After that it stops. I get Gracie back to sleep and step into the kitchen where the little red light is blinking on the machine, but nothing has been recorded except a hissing silence. I delete the wordless messages, switch the ringer on the phone to *off*. It feels like I'm switching off the life support system for him, for the one I love more than anyone, more than life itself. I grit my teeth, try to keep from crying, force myself to not pick up the phone and call him again as I so desperately want to, beg him in my mind not to call here again tonight. He doesn't.

I'm edgy all the time now. Bill returns and I wonder if he'll find it as easy to detect what's going on as my four-year-old daughter did. But no, poor gullible Bill doesn't have the slightest idea. I worry what Gracie might blurt out at the dinner table some evening, but realize that Bill would never believe it anyway. *Mommy and that boy who shovels the snow took their clothes off and played grown-up games on the floor in the living room one night. I saw them.* His wife brought her eleven-year-old student into the house and fucked him on the living room carpet and was so unaware of anything that she didn't realize her daughter had awakened, gotten out of bed and was watching them? Ridiculous. There's never been a hint of anything untoward about his wife, not one single thing in ten years, and now *this?* He'd think it was like the McMartin Preschool case years ago, when children were encouraged to tell tales of orgies and devil worshipping going on in their classes. Those manipulated children were believed, for a while. But no one would believe Gracie's story about Mommy, Ms. Straw, *Mo-na*, certainly not Bill, dear Bill, trusting Bill with his much younger wife who he believes could never betray him. Bill, who has lost most of his illusions over the years but not the one about Mona, perfect little Mona. *You just had a dream, honey.*

When I'm with Bill at night I start things sexually now. Even as I feel nauseous and hysterical, keep my eyes closed, my mind far away, I'm enthusiastic in bed, creative, fun. It's my way of apologizing to him. I pretend that I've sat down with him and confessed everything, every single thing I've done, and he's taken me in his arms and told me he forgives me and that we'll speak no more of it, darling. Yes, he's forgiven me, in his heart he has, in his heart he knows something's wrong but he forgives me because he's always forgiven me everything and I love him for it, I love him even as I can't stand him anymore, his sagging jowls, his listless attempts at lovemaking. He can barely manage to finish sexually once and then can't get it up again for days. It's pathetically easy to please him in bed, to exhaust him. It takes only minutes. Bill's fifty but looks fifty-five, acts sixty. I can't live like this. But I must live like this.

And so when the school year starts again Connor and I go to motels.

It isn't easy. It's hard to even find time to talk to him about it, furtive whispers in the few minutes no one else is in the room at the end of fourth period. I've stopped the lunchtime movie watching, told Connor he must go play with the other kids, we don't dare let anyone start to imagine there's anything between us. He sulks but understands. The after-school tutoring group continues but I'm careful to show Connor no more attention than Lauren or Richard or Kylie or any of the kids who appear for extra help. Once when he's sitting beside me getting directions on how to do a math problem he moves his hand, which is hidden from the others by my big teacher's desk, onto my own. I pull my hand away as if he'd spat on it, shoot him a fierce look. He doesn't do it again. Instead we arrange that I'll pick him up on this corner, that corner, the middle of such-and-such block. Always different pick-up points, in different directions, as far away as I can reasonably expect him to be able to walk. I find a new day care for Gracie just across the street from the old one which will keep her an hour longer than the other. If I rush out of school at the end of the day, drive aimlessly for a few minutes or pick up a few groceries and then go pick up Connor wherever he is, take him to wherever we're going, spend an hour with him there, I can still be back before the day care closes and before Bill's home. But it's difficult, looking up all these cheap motels so I know where to drive us and don't waste any of the time we have together. The Sleepy Bear Lodge, the Skyview Inn, Motel 6, Super 8, all in Maryland, northern Virginia, D.C. itself. We never use the subway; I feel safer and more in control driving my car, and anyway we need places sufficiently out of the way that there's no Metro stop for them. The first few times I have him hide in the vehicle and check in as a single, but then decide we're more liable to attract attention by getting caught at that than if I simply sign us in as a party of two, mother and son: "Just passing through. My boy is in the car." Connor stays in the car always, never meets anyone at these run-down places. Two beds are in the room when I sign us in as two and they're smaller but it's better, we're not breaking any motel rules, not sneaking in any unpaid guests. We're honest and respectable. I use a different name each time, of course. I pay cash, of course. Even that's difficult. I have my own bank account along with Bill's and my various joint ones, but it's not terribly large and dropping fifty or sixty dollars a couple of times a week on motel rooms quickly adds up. But the thing I fear most, that's in the back of my mind always, is if I were to walk into the office of a motel and find behind the counter someone I know. But we generally drive ten or twenty miles out of Silver Spring and I know no one who works in any motel, anyway. And I do have a story prepared. The room isn't for me, it's for a friend coming in from out of town tonight. I would make the reservation, tell them to expect my friend later that evening. The friend would never show. Connor and I would drive back home.

At first Connor is tremendously excited simply to see different motel rooms. He's hardly ever stayed in a motel, he says. "Just once, when my dad took me to a baseball game in Boston. I was really little." He's interested in the ice machines outside, the little cakes of soap in their paper wrappers, the toilet paper folded just so on the roll, the towels, the TVs. ("Hey, Mona!"—he's growing more comfortable with my name—"look, they have HBO!") But soon enough ("We don't have much time, Connor, sweetheart"), I have him choose which bed we'll use. Each time I teach him patiently how to slow down, how to be a partner, a *lover*, rather than an overexcited boy. He learns quickly. He's wonderful, wonderful beyond words. But soon, terribly soon it's over, each time it's over, I look at my watch and realize that if I'm going to get back in time to pick up Gracie we have to go in the next half-hour, twenty minutes, ten minutes.

Part of me hates all this. Hates the frantic darting around, the secretiveness, the slow driving to a certain corner, nerves jumping under my skin, hoping Connor didn't get confused about where he's supposed to be standing—that happens once, I never find him, I'm crushed, heartbroken, wail in tear-filled frustration and beat my hands on the steering wheel while I circle, circle, circle, and all the time (I learn from him later) he's two blocks over, lost, panicked, needing me and I'm not there. But he's there, I wave casually, pull over, he gets in as quickly as he can, just as I've told him to, I pull away fast but not too fast. I don't have him hide on the car floor or anything melodramatic like that. We've already got our story. I was giving him a ride, that's all. I happened to see him and he was going to (fill in blank depending on what direction we went that day) and I stopped to give him a ride, nothing more. Ms. Straw is never not helpful to her students. Everyone knows that. We never touch each other in the car, not even to hold hands. That's a firm rule. It's good that Mr. Blue is so often not home, so inattentive to his son when he is. Excuses with him are easy for Connor—he was at a movie, he was at a friend's house. His dad doesn't care, never checks on anything. It's terrible of me to think of myself as grateful to him, but in an ironic way I am. Connor doesn't need his useless violent dad for anything, anyway. Connor needs *me*.

Still, part of me hates this. I want to bring Connor into my life, into my family, make him proudly and beautifully part of the Mona Straw everyone sees and knows and admires. But it isn't possible. And so it's dirty motel rooms, grimy doorknobs, sheets that reek of bleach, and always the infernal time limit, the ticking of the clock. Usually by the time we're in the room we have an hour, an hour and a quarter. Ninety minutes is heaven. Once there's light traffic and the motel is one of the closer ones we've ever used and we have two full hours. We make love twice, watch the last few minutes of *Brute Force* with Burt Lancaster on TV, shower luxuriously together, and I still make it to Gracie's day care on time. It's one of the most wonderful days we've ever had.

Often only once a week with him. Sometimes twice. Never more than that. I can't possibly keep my other life together if we do this more than twice a week. Grocery shopping, house cleaning, making dinner, taking care of Gracie, building lesson plans and grading papers. And I know I can't let things fall apart, that I must keep up this other life, be the exemplary wife and mother and teacher that I am. It's vital to not let those things slip. They me sane, keep me knowing that *Mona Straw* still exists even if she's taken over for hours sometimes by this frenzied stranger, this frantic hysterical madwoman who can think of nothing but making love again and again to her young boyfriend in the afternoon, touching him, pulling, sucking, our skins slapping together, shrieking with joy with him. How new everything is to him, how fresh and awe-inspiring and unimaginable. I can see it through his eyes, imagine what it's like for him to be with me, so different from my own puzzling and disappointing first experiences with sex. His energy and enthusiasm are boundless. He'll try anything that involves us touching each other in a new way. His excitement fuels mine. But afterwards is even better, our hair blending together on a single pillow, arms and hips and legs pushed together in the narrow bed, hands clasped, breathing, staring at the ceiling.

Once he asks, "Have you ever done this with anyone else?"

I glance at him. "Of course I have, sweetheart. I'm married. I have a daughter."

"I mean like this."

"In motel rooms?"

"With a guy. Not your husband."

I turn to him, rest my head on my elbow, dangle my hair in his face. "No. Never."

"Really?"

"Never."

"I mean, it's okay. It doesn't matter. I'm just curious."

"Never, sweetheart."

He looks away, is silent for a while. Then: "Mona, is it normal to jack off every day?"

"Oh, I'm sure it's normal, Connor."

"Twice a day?"

I chuckle, then shrug. "I wouldn't worry about it. You're young and energetic."

"I think about you when I do it."

"Thank you."

"But it's not like really being with you."

"No. There's nothing like being with someone you love."

He's silent for a moment. Then: "So you've never done it with one of your students before?"

"Never." I grin and kiss him. "You're my first. My first and only."

He seems to think about it. "Why me?"

He looks at me. We look at each other. I don't really know how to answer. "People fall in love, Connor, that's all. There's no explaining it."

"Are you in love with your husband?"

His voice is soft, open, not accusing. He just wants to know, with the innocence of any young kid.

"I used to be." I play with his nipples. "I love him. I do. I care about Bill. Very much. But I don't feel about him the way I feel about you."

"You fell in love with him and then you fell out of love with him?"

I think. "Well, it took a long time. But something like that. Yeah."

"Will you fall out of love with me, Mona?"

"Oh, Connor, no." I press myself to him. "I'll always love you, Connor. Always."

"Promise?"

"Promise. You know what'll happen, though? *You'll* fall out of love with *me.*"

He shakes his head vehemently. "Nuh-uh."

"You will. You'll start to notice all these pretty girls your own age and you'll decide you don't need some stinking old woman in your life anymore."

"*No.*" He holds me close, tight, buries his face in my breasts. "You're not old. You're not stinking."

"I will be someday, though. I'll be old and wrinkly and fat and my boobs will sag."

"No. You'll always be beautiful. *Always.*" He's crying, I realize. Wetness covers my chest.

"Sweetheart, sweetheart," I say, taking his face in my hands, kissing his salty wet eyes, "calm down. I'm here. We're here together, right where we want to be. Nothing else matters."

His voice cracks. "I don't want things to change. Ever. Between us."

I stroke his hair, pressing his damp face against my chest again. "Oh, Connor," I whisper, "oh, sweetheart, my baby, my love, my true love, neither do I. Neither do I."

classroom, didn't try to whisper something to me after class after the other children had gone.

Something darkens and sinks inside me. The day is bright but the light seems somehow wrong to me, glaring, accusing. Like the light on some alien planet, not meant for humans to see. Poisonous, deadly. I wonder if Connor is thinking of me at all as he runs up and down the field, if I cross his mind, if there's some part of him that wishes he could be with me right now or if he's forgotten all about what we are to each other. When I take him aside the next day and tell him what corner to meet me on that afternoon, he says casually—not negatively but casually, as if it's of no importance—"Oh, okay." When I pull up to him on the sidewalk and he sees me his face doesn't light up, it doesn't become suffused with that apple-glow in the way it did in our dozen or more earlier sessions. He smiles, that's all, gets in. Doesn't say a word. Doesn't ask what motel we're going to, how close it is, doesn't ask little-boy questions about anything we're passing by on the way there. I feel something's changed between us but I'm afraid to ask what, afraid to even breathe a suggestion to him that his behavior around me seems different. When we get to the room (the "Kings Court Motel"), he jumps on one of the beds, grabs the TV remote and switches on the set, all but ignoring me.

"Baby," I say, dropping down beside him, taking the remote from his hand and switching it off, "we don't have much time."

"Oh, okay."

Not unpleasant. Not frowning or complaining. And once we're making love it's just as it's always been, wonderful, indescribable, yet even now something's subtly altered. I

16

Things begin to change.

It starts with the coming of early spring, the weather turning from cold to cool. Soon I don't see Connor's big coat anymore. Instead he wears a yellow sweater some days, a brown hoodie another. He begins talking more with the other boys in the class, hanging out with them at lunchtime. Once I'm on duty and hope to talk to him a little, maybe walk up to him with his book in his hand and say, "Whatcha readin', Connor?" But instead he's on the athletic fields playing soccer. I almost call him over. I want to stand close to him, see the sweat on his face and in his hair, breathe in his active boy-smell, but I know not to. Instead I watch him running up the field with the ball, away from me, away from *us*, driving straight to the goal. He kicks and scores. His friends yell and whoop and congratulate him.

I know he needs time with kids his age. I know he needs a chance to be a boy. Yet I feel a terrible sadness watching him. He never once asked me that day if we could spend time together, didn't plead to be allowed to watch a movie in my straddle him and stroke his chest and dangle my hair playfully in his face and move rhythmically with him inside me and he doesn't *respond*. He's there, he thrusts himself into me, his hands are warm on my hips, he smiles when I say anything to him, but his eyes are somehow vacant. And now when we finish once he doesn't ask to do it again, instead allowing me to hold him for a few minutes and then saying he has a lot of homework to do and we should get back.

"Connor, sweetheart, we have time, just a few more minutes."

But it could be my imagination. He's still pleasant, smiling, fun. We still talk, we still make jokes, act silly.

"Mona?" he asks once in bed. "Do you think that Rick and Ilsa had sex in *Casablanca?*"

"I'm sure they did, baby."

"What about John and Frances in *To Catch a Thief?*"

"Cary Grant and Grace Kelly? They'd better have! I'd have sex with either one of them."

Connor laughs, the old laugh, the high boy-giggle I know. "You'd have sex with a lady?"

"I'll bet *you'd* have sex with her if she let you."

"Well, yeah," he says, running his finger from my nipples to my navel, "but I'd think about you when I was doing it."

We laugh, we roll around the bed, everything is as before. But such moments seem to happen with decreasing frequency. Connor grows ever more quiet, even now, at times, moody. I try not to become hysterical about this, try to keep from thinking that he's losing interest, that I'm losing *him*. There's no evidence of it, after all. He's a boy. He's supposed to be moody sometimes. It just means he's grown more comfortable with me, that's all, he feels he can express more of his real self around me, be more natural and easy with me. At times after we finish I hold him, run my hand over his hair as I did that first time, the first time I knew there was something unexplored and magical between us, and ask him how he's doing, how his life is—"Are you happy, Connor? With me? With everything?" And we have beautiful heart-to-heart talks, just the two of us, about his fears, his joys, his sadnesses.

One rain-filled afternoon he tells me how much he misses his mother. "Even though I never knew her. Isn't that weird, to miss somebody you never knew?"

"It's not weird, sweetheart." I stroke his hair. "She died when you were…?"

"Two."

"Two."

"I don't remember her. I've tried. It's like sometimes I think I can almost hear her voice or, like, see her or something like that. But it always goes away."

"I'm sorry, sweetie. I wish I could make it better."

We sit listening to the rain outside the dirty motel room and I wait for him to say something like *You always make everything better, Mona,* but he doesn't. He remains wordless, motionless, accepting my touch but not reciprocating. After a while when it's nearly time to leave he gets up and goes to the bathroom, turns on the shower without me, doesn't invite me in. I shower alone after he's done and we drive back to the city in silence.

Another time there's a bruise on his left bicep, a purple and yellow stain.

"Connor," I say carefully, touching it softly around the edges with my finger, "does your dad hit you?"

He looks away.

"You can tell me, Connor."

After a long time he says, "I guess. I mean, sort of."

"Sort of?"

He shrugs. "He pushes me sometimes. When he's drunk."

"Oh, Connor." I nuzzle him. It crosses my mind that I would call child protective services, but then it crosses my mind that of course I can't do any such thing. I hate Connor's father even more now. "Connor, I'm so sorry."

I become aware of a new element only gradually, and at first I'm unable to believe it. It begins at the afternoon dance we have in March, to celebrate the coming of spring. The eleven- and twelve-year-olds are herded into the school's gym one afternoon. We on the staff have decorated it with streamers and balloons and Dave Tisdale, the science teacher, serves as DJ. There's punch and cookies in the back of the hall. The lights are turned low—slightly low, at least. It's a socialization exercise, we do it twice a year at Cutts. It's always cute to watch the young boys nervously approach the girls, the girls hiding in packs so as not to be invited out to the dance floor—for a while, anyway. After a few songs their courage grows stronger and they largely separate, make themselves available, and soon the floor is covered with clumsy middle-schoolers dancing to rock music.

Connor stays in the back, playing checkers with the other boys too shy to become part of the social swim. I watch him, wish I could walk over to him, take his hand, walk out to the dance floor and embrace him in a slow dance no matter what music is playing. I wish I could stroke him, kiss him, announce to everyone there what we are, how we have something between us that they can never understand, that we love each other. But no. Instead I sit there with several other teachers blandly chaperoning, never actually doing anything except once when I stand and wander the perimeter for a few minutes, saying hi to kids, letting them know I'm here.

But when I turn to go back to my spot I'm confronted with an astonishing sight.

Connor, Connor Blue, my love, my lover, is walking nervously out onto the dance floor just in front of my quiet little book-reading student Kylie McCloud.

A fast song has started and they gyrate as best they can. I'm surprised to see Connor dancing but I'm flabbergasted to see Kylie, backward shy Kylie, out there. Neither of them can dance at all but of course that makes no difference, it's not the point. Kylie's short mousy hair bounces, her glasses slip down her nose as they always do, she watches her dance partner with her head slightly uptilted and her mouth open a little. I wonder if she needs her asthma inhaler. At this moment I couldn't be prouder of Connor, taking the little girl no one likes and making her a part of things.

When the dance is over Kylie returns to her seat and picks up her book as always, buries her nose in it as always. But that's all right. She can go home and tell her mom that she danced at the dance, that a boy asked her and she got up and did it. I'm happy for her, so happy. But I'm even more surprised when Connor, having wandered around the back of the hall with the other boys for a few songs, steps up to Kylie again. This time I see him ask her. Looking down her nose at him she's obviously surprised, possibly having suspected that the earlier dance had been from pity, that he'd felt sorry for her. I actually see her point at her own chest: *Me?* Connor nods, God bless him, and they have another go on the dance floor. All the teachers are remarking on it: *Oh my God, look at that, that's so cute!*

They end up spending much of the rest of the dance together, to my—and everyone else's—amazement. They dance again and again. They go together to the punch bowl, the ever-gallant Connor serving her a glass of punch. I can just read her lips when she says *Thank you* and takes the glass. I hope she doesn't drop it, spill it all over herself or something else equally clumsy, equally Kylie. Let this go well for her, I think. Let it be magic.

Late in the hour-long dance Dave Tisdale puts on a slow song. I don't even know what it is, I don't know young people's music. But the sound is soft, the beat slow. It's the first such he's played. Connor and Kylie are standing on the sideline with most of the other kids, nervously considering matters. There are two couples already on the floor, both pairings of longtime friends. Other boys start speaking to other girls, head hesitantly out to the floor, moving as if they're afraid there may be land mines near. Finally, yes, Connor steps forward—he takes Kylie's hand—and he leads her to an open spot, puts his palms gently on her waist. For a moment she stands with her arms frozen at her sides, doesn't seem to know what to do. Finally Connor starts to move a little, to circle slowly with her, and her hands flutter helplessly in the air until finally they move to his shoulders and then stay there, never move an inch. She's stiff, holds herself as far as she possibly can from him. But when the song is done she's danced a slow dance with a boy. All of the teachers are touched. I find myself wanting to cry, to run onto the floor and thank Connor for being just as special as I always knew he was.

And the next day it's Connor and Kylie who are the item, the talk of the class. Connor takes it well, grinning and blushing, while Kylie actually raises her head out of her book for a while, smiling and laughing at the first teasing she's ever received that isn't malicious and hurtful. If anything, the girls in school seem impressed with her, as if they just discovered hidden resources in this bashful bookworm—after all, many of *them* didn't slow dance.

After fourth period I stand at the door as the kids run out to lunch and I stop Connor. We're not alone, there are still a couple of kids in the room, but what I have to say isn't private. "Connor, I'm so proud of you," I say, smiling down at him.

"For what?"

I nod toward Kylie, who is still at her desk, reading. "You know."

"Oh. Yeah. Hey, Kylie!" he calls, looking around me. "C'mon, it's lunchtime."

Her head pops up as if she's just pulled herself from a dream.

"Huh? Oh, okay." She gathers her things and follows Connor out of the room. "Bye, Ms. Straw."

"Bye, Kylie. Have a nice lunch."

"Thank you!"

They eat together, sitting in the spring sunshine with their brown paper bags and sandwiches and juice boxes. I watch them from my classroom window curiously. It appears that he actually likes her. They're talking about her book, whatever book she's reading, she holds it up for him to see and they look at it together. They laugh about something. I've never seen Kylie's face so animated, so happy.

"I think it's really nice, you spending time with Kylie," I say later, in that week's motel room bed.

He doesn't respond.

"I mean it," I say. "You're very gallant. But, sweetheart, can I make a suggestion?"

"What?"

"Don't be *too* friendly with her. Don't lead her on."

"Lead her on?"

"You know, don't act as if you really want to be her boyfriend or something."

"Why not?"

"You could hurt her *feelings*, Connor."

He's silent for a moment.

"I like her," he says at last.

"Do you?"

"She's actually really smart."

"Oh?"

"You just have to get to know her. She's shy."

They take to spending their lunch hours together every day. Every day I'm left in the classroom, watching them. They don't sit close, they don't touch. They're eleven, after all. But they spend enough time together that the other kids tease them: *CON-ner 'n' KY-lie, sittin' in a tree! K-I-S-S-I-N-G!* Yet it's all good-natured ribbing. Their classmates seem genuinely happy at their relationship, especially with Kylie's sudden blossoming. The verbal abuse of the girl drops quickly away amidst admiring whispers: *Kylie has a boyfriend!* I still have to constantly tell her to get her nose out of her book during class, and she still seems oblivious to her surroundings much of the time, but during lunch she's animated, smiling, seemingly where she wants to be when she's with Connor Blue, just as I am.

"Mona?" Another week, another motel room bed.

"Mm?"

Silence.

"What, sweetheart?"

He turns away. I stroke his back lightly.

"Do you—do you think that we're dirty?"

"Dirty? What do you mean?"

"What we do together. Are we dirty?"

"I don't understand."

"Sometimes I think what we do together is dirty."

I kiss the back of his neck. "What we do together is natural, Connor. Everybody does it."

His silence is discontented. I can feel it.

"Sweetheart, what? What's bothering you?"

"It just seems dirty," he says.

"You never said it seemed dirty before."

"I know."

"So why is it dirty now?"

"I don't know." He sighs and pulls away from me.

"Connor, I love you." I tousle his hair. "There's nothing dirty about love."

"I guess."

I try to hold down a sour ball of panic that I can feel building in me, in my stomach, my throat.

"Connor, does this have something to do with Kylie?"

"No."

"You sure?"

"Yes."

"I'm happy you two are friends, sweetheart. I really am. I think it's cute."

"Don't say 'cute'."

"What?"

"You make it sound like I'm a baby."

"Honey, come on. You know I didn't mean it like that."

"I guess."

"Connor, what's wrong? Please. Tell me."

"Nothing's wrong."

"I think there is. Because it seems like you've been changing, sweetheart, ever since you got to know Kylie. Even before. But especially since then."

"I'm not changing."

"You don't seem as happy as you used to. Don't you know how much I love you?"

"Yes."

"Don't you like what we do together? You sure act like you do. When we're doing it, I mean."

Silence. Finally he sits up, facing away from me.

"I'm not sure I can come next week," he says finally. "I have a big paper for Mr. Thorndyke that'll take me every day to work on after school."

I prop myself up on my elbow, look at his pale back.

"Can't even spare an hour?" I say.

"I don't think so. I'll let you know."

I run my finger along his spine, all the way to his bottom.

"Connor, if you're going to dump a girl you should do it *before* you make love to her, not after."

He looks back. "I'm not dumping you."

"Really?"

He turns away again. "I'm just busy."

"Busy with Kylie?"

"Busy with *school.*"

I scoot myself close to him, snake my arm around him, stroke his thigh, reach for his penis and grasp it.

"Don't," he says, pushing my hand away.

"Connor, not fifteen minutes ago..."

"I *know* what I did fifteen minutes ago."

"Then what's wrong?"

"I just...I don't know."

I study him. "Connor, do you have any idea what I have to go through to get us together in these motel rooms? Do you? How hard it is? To find places that we can use? To arrange everything? To pay for everything? Do you know how much risk I put myself in, doing all this? And I do it for *you.* It's all for you."

"I think you get something out of it."

"I get your *come*," I say, sitting up, my heart pumping. I try to keep my voice low, even. "It's running down my leg right now. Want to see it?"

"No."

"You put it there. You put it there and then a few minutes later you tell me you don't want to see me anymore."

"I just said *next week.*"

We sit in angry silence for a while.

Finally Connor stands, looks at me. "I'm going to take a shower," he says.

"Because you're dirty? With me? You have *me* on you?"

He glances at me, then away.

"Connor, if you keep spending time with Kylie and you date her and all that, what do you think will eventually happen?"

"What do you mean?"

"Between you two. In a few years."

"I don't know."

"You'll end up doing the same 'dirty' things we do together. That's what will happen."

"That's different."

"How is it different?"

"We're not even…Mona, we're not…we're just kids! We just read together and talk about—about *books* and stuff. Classes. Teachers."

"Oh? What do you say about me?"

"Nothing."

"You sure?"

"We don't talk about you. I mean, Kylie said she likes you. As a teacher. She thinks you're a good teacher."

"Do you think I'm a good teacher?"

"I don't know."

"Connor, have you kissed Kylie?"

"No." He shrugs, then says: "Not really. After school a couple of days ago she asked me if I'd ever kissed a girl."

"And what did you say to that?"

"I said I had once. Then I…I don't know, I asked if I could kiss her."

"Why?"

"'Cuz I like her."

"And did you? Kiss her?"

He glances at me, embarrassed. "She said I could kiss her on the cheek. So I did."

I laugh.

"And then she kissed me on the cheek back."

"How sweet. I mean it. Really sweet."

"You're talking like I'm a baby again."

"Come back to bed, sweetheart. I'll show you how much of a baby I think you are."

"No."

I pat the mattress beside me. "C'mere."

"I don't want to."

"Yes, you do. *He* does." I point at his slowly rising erection.

"Mona…"

"Just come to *bed*. We'll sort out the rest later." I hold out my hand, palm up. "Come on, Connor," I say softly. "I need you to be a man now."

He moves reluctantly toward me, but he moves. He reaches out his hand and I grab it, pull him onto the bed. In a moment we're wrestling and giggling and kissing and everything is fine, just fine, there's nothing wrong, nothing.

17

Life blurs. Increasingly I'm an automaton with Gracie, with Bill. I'm there but I'm not. It's the same with classes, except the one Connor is in. And even then there's an unreality to all the other kids, to talking about some great writer's story, to diagramming a sentence on the board. I manage to get through it, through everything, most people don't know there's anything wrong at all. Gracie never again says anything about the boy who shovels the snow and she seems to have forgotten him. Bill and I just go on as people who have been married for a decade and have a child go on. But I don't know how long it can last. I'm dead inside whenever I'm not with Connor. I puff myself up with personal pep talks and make sure that I dress nicely and I resolve to smile smile *smile* but I'm dead inside. Joyful spring blossoms are everywhere, mocking me, blue spring skies berate me, cool April breezes call me worthless, not fit to live. I know what I am. I know what I've done, what I'm doing. I know that nobody else on earth would ever understand. But I also know that I'm a good mother, a good wife. I'm having an affair with a boy but I am a good wife to Bill, he's proud of me, he loves me. He's curious about my moodiness sometimes, maybe a little concerned, but he supports me, cheers me on, doesn't ask questions, lets me live my life. He tells me how sexy I am when I wear a low-cut black dress to one of his employer's functions, tells me how he saw the other guys checking me out and he's right, they were. I keep a good home for him. I take care of our child. He can't ask for more from his wife, he wouldn't dream of it.

And school? I still run the afternoon tutoring group. I'm not paid anything extra for this, I just do it. I make the calls home when Richard Broad's behavior has been disruptive, I make the calls home when he's done well that day. I help Kevin Simmons, who has a slight speech impediment, with his pronunciations. I teach Cheryl Milton how to outline the events in a chapter so that she can remember what happened in the book. I arrange to have Andrew Harrington, who always struggles with English, tested for dyslexia, which it turns out he has, and I help set up an enhanced program for him with a private specialist. I create original assignments, allow my students to express themselves in different ways, respond to a book or story or poem through art or music or their own creative writing. My classes are fun in the best ways. Not everything works, my lessons are sometimes a little sloppy, but engagingly so, in a manner that makes kids want to come into the room and learn. Other teachers tell me that students enter their classes talking excitedly about mine. Even Estelle Higgins is friendly with me again. I watch kids, so many kids get better at reading and writing, grow stronger and more self-confident, after I've spent time with them. I'm a gifted teacher, I know. Few others, even the most experienced and trained, can do what Ms. Straw does in the classroom. I know that. And I know that none of it would count for anything if the truth came out, the secret. One student among the hundreds I've taught and tutored and counseled and befriended. I would be a monster beyond the pale of humanity, shunned, imprisoned, wished hanged or gassed or shot. And yet I know that unless Connor is near me I'm already beyond all hope of redemption, I'm dead inside, completely and utterly dead.

***

"Mona?"

"Mm?" I snuggle against him.

"Who's your family? I mean, your parents and stuff?"

I look at him. "Well," I say, "my parents are both dead. I don't have any other relatives. Bill and Gracie are my family. And you."

"Don't you have any brothers or sisters?"

"No." And yet, though I never talk about this to anyone, I find myself saying, "I had a brother once."

"What happened to him?"

"He died, honey."

"I'm sorry."

"It was a long time ago."

"How old was he when he died?"

"Twelve."

"How old were you?"

"Twelve." When he looks at me curiously I add, "We were twins."

"You had a twin?"

"Mm-hm."

He's silent for a while. Finally: "What was his name?"

"His name was Michael." It sounds strange in my mouth. Another silence.

"What was that like?" he says at last. "Having a twin?"

I touch his chest, his ribs. "Oh, it's so long ago, sweetheart, I don't even remember."

***

That night the dream again, the dream I used to have when I was a girl: naked before a mirror, one-half of my body gone, balanced on one leg, a single arm, half a head—one eye, one ear, a half-mouth. I wake up weeping.

***

One afternoon Kylie is the last student left in the afternoon study period. The pale little girl sits next to me at my desk while I help her grasp the difference between an adjective and an adverb. When we're done she looks at me with her head tilted back to see through her glasses and says, "Ms. Straw?"

"Yes, Kylie?"

"Do you think I'm too young to have a boyfriend?"

I smile. "What makes you ask that?"

"It's what my mom says. She likes Connor but she thinks I'm too young to have a boyfriend."

"Your mom has met Connor?"

"Mm-hm. He came over on Saturday. We watched TV." Her voice is as tiny as she is. It has a perpetually congested sound, as if her nose is always stuffed up. No doubt it's the result of her asthma.

"Did you?"

"Connor likes old movies. We watched one called *Sorry, Wrong Number*. It was good. It was scary. And we watched cartoons."

"That sounds like a great time, Kylie."

"My mom made popcorn and everything."

"Wow." I smile. "But she thinks you're too young to have a boyfriend?"

"Yeah." She makes a sour face. "He can only come over when she's there."

"Well, that's not so bad. At least he can visit you."

"I can't go to his house, though."

"Well, your mom feels protective. This is all pretty new for her, Kylie. And for you too."

She glances at me mischievously and then whispers: "Can I tell you a secret?"

I lean to her and whisper in return, "Sure."

It takes her a minute to get it out. "He kissed me."

"He did?"

"Mm-hm." She nods. "Right here." She puts her finger on her right cheek.

"Wow. That's pretty special."

"I kissed him, too."

"Where?"

"On his cheek. Right here." She illustrates on her own cheek.

"Wow."

She meets my eyes for a second, then giggles and turns away, blushing.

"But you'll be careful, right?" I ask her.

"What do you mean?"

"Well, Kylie, I'm sure your mother has told you about boys, right?"

"A little."

"Sometimes they can get...aggressive. You know what I mean?"

"No."

"Well...pushy. Like maybe they want to do something with you that you don't want to do and they try to pressure you to do it."

"Like what?"

"Well, like kissing, if you don't want to kiss."

"I like kissing."

"I'm sure you do. But only on the cheek, right? What if a boy wanted to kiss you somewhere else?"

She makes a little fist. "I'd bop him one."

I laugh. "It can be different, though, if you're with a boy you like. What if Connor tried to kiss you somewhere else?"

"He wouldn't do that. He's nice."

"Well, he's a boy. That's what I mean. Boys can get pushy. That's what your mom is worried about. He might..." I'm not sure what I'm saying, but somehow it comes out. "He might try to kiss you on the mouth. Or he might try to touch you. You know, in other ways than you touch when you're dancing. He might put his hands on your chest or your bottom."

"Why?"

"Well, boys like to do that with girls. He might even want you to take your clothes off."

"Connor would do that?"

"All I'm saying is that Connor is a boy and they sometimes push things with girls. So you have to be careful. And I've heard that Connor…" The words rush forth. "I've heard that he—he's known a lot of girls. That he has a lot of experience with them."

"He does?"

"That's what I've heard. He's done a lot of things with girls."

"Really? With their clothes off?"

"Well, I don't know about that," I say, "but I just think he knows a lot about girls, that's all. So it's good that you're careful with him. You should always be careful around Connor. Always make sure that your mom's there."

The girl looks troubled. At last she rises from her chair. "Thanks, Ms. Straw."

"I'm not saying don't see him, Kylie. I'm just saying be careful."

She nods. "Okay." She gathers her things and moves quietly toward the door. She takes one more concerned look at me and then steps out.

***

It's lunchtime the next day and Connor suddenly comes into the room and shuts the door hard behind him. I look up.

"Connor, what are you doing? Open the door, please."

"What did you say to Kylie?"

"What?"

His eyes are furious. "Kylie. What did you say to her?"

"I didn't say anything to Kylie."

"Liar. You're a liar. You said something to her. She told me you did."

"Connor, I just—I just reinforced what her mother had said. About being careful around boys."

"Why is it your business?"

"Because she's my student. I care about her. I don't want her to get into any trouble."

"With me? Is that what you mean?"

"Connor…" I get up from the desk, lean in front of it. "Sweetheart, she's a little girl. I know you and she are the same age but she's really much younger than you. You understand that, don't you?"

"I know."

"You aren't expecting to do with her what you do with me, are you?"

"*No.*" He scowls. "I don't even think about that. You're dirty."

"Connor, open the door."

"Why?"

"Because I asked you to."

"You *told* me to."

I sigh loudly. "Connor, would you *please* open the door?"

But instead of opening it he reaches over and twists the slender stick that closes the blinds.

"Connor, what in the world are you doing?" I march authoritatively up to him, expect him to be intimidated enough to move away from the door. But he stands his ground.

"You scared Kylie on purpose. You're jealous."

I chuckled. "I'm jealous of Kylie McCloud? Connor, do you hear what you're saying?"

"I like her better than I like you."

My jaw drops. I feel it drop.

"Connor...sweetheart..."

I see tears spring to his eyes. "I don't know how to *act* around her. I feel like I'm twenty years older than her. I feel like I'm with a little kid. But I really *like* her."

"That's wonderful. I've told you it's wonderful. I'm happy you're together."

"You said it was *cute,*" he spits. "Like I'm a little boy."

"Connor, you *are* eleven, you know."

"You don't act like it when we're at the motel."

"You never complained."

"It's wrong. It's dirty. You're not supposed to do those things with a little kid."

"Oh, you're a little kid now? All these months we've been doing what we do together and suddenly you're a little kid?"

"You don't understand."

"Connor, please open the door. We shouldn't be caught alone together. People may get ideas."

"So?" He looks defiantly at me. "You're the one who'll get in trouble, not me."

"Connor—I can't believe you're speaking to me like this. Sweetheart..."

"I can get you *fired*. Right now. All I have to do is scream."

"Connor..." Beads of perspiration run down my neck. My heart pounds.

"I can go to the principal's office and tell him *everything.*"

I try to sound calm, reasonable, the adult in charge. "Mr. Lewis? Do you think he'd believe you, Connor?"

"I'd make him believe me. I could tell him about the motels we go to. About how you plan where to pick me up every time."

"He'll never believe any of that, Connor." I'm not sure that I do myself.

"I can tell him how you started with me in your house. Touching me. Then coming into the bathroom and taking my clothes off."

"You don't have any evidence that any of that happened, Connor."

"I can tell him what you look like *naked.*"

"Do you think Mr. Lewis has seen me naked? How would he know you were telling the truth?"

"They'd get a police lady to look. When they *arrest* you."

I feel myself deflating, my vision going dark. All I can think of to say is, "Connor, I love you. I've tried to make things special between us. I'm sorry if I've done the wrong thing. I really am. We can stop if you want. We won't do it anymore."

He frowns, looks at the floor, wipes his eyes with his palms.

"I have a family, Connor. A husband. My daughter is four years old. Think of what would happen to them. And to my classes. All the kids."

He doesn't meet my eyes, just looks at the floor.

"Just don't scare Kylie again," he says.

"I won't. I promise. I'm sorry, sweetheart. I'm so sorry."

Finally he looks up and nods. He turns to the door, twists the knob.

"Connor?"

"What?"

I look at him. "Are we meeting this afternoon, Connor?"

He stands there a long time. Finally he says, "Yeah. Sure. Whatever."

***

Once I'm stepping into the grocery store with Gracie as Mr. Blue is stepping out. He has on his usual faded denim. He smells of cigarettes and alcohol.

"Hello, Mr. Blue," I say.

"Hey. Mrs.—Straw, right?"

"Ms. Yes."

"Connor's teacher. Hey, he's doin' pretty good this year."

"Yes, he is. He's a good boy, Mr. Blue."

He continues out to the parking lot, gets into his pickup, and drives away. It's the last time I ever see him.

18

I throw myself ever more deeply into my job, stay later hours, bring more work home, call more parents. Nothing works. None of this is real to me anymore. I'm dead, dead inside, there's only Connor and every lunch period I watch him moving farther and farther from me. He doesn't want to talk to me. He spends his lunchtimes with Kylie McCloud. On nice days they sit out on the grass reading books, sometimes close enough together that their shoulders touch or their shoes. It's accepted among the other kids that Connor and Kylie are now a couple, the first real couple in their grade. They're not like most kids who become couples, who claim to be going steady but who rarely actually talk to each other. This is not a pretend relationship. They're actually together, at least as friends. Connor sits there reading an Alfred Hitchcock paperback while Kylie leans over one of her big fantasy books. Once, my heart dying, I walk outside where they are, step up to them and say, "Hi Connor, hi Kylie. Whatcha readin'?" Kylie smiles up at me, tilting her head back to see me through the glasses that have slid down her nose, and shows me the book, tells me all about it. Connor merely glares at me. I smile, tell them to enjoy themselves, slink away like a criminal.

I can hardly even remember the first times, months and months ago now, when everything was fresh and new and his eyes opened wide with every new sight and sensation. When he was innocent. He's not innocent anymore. He's grown bored with me. What we do is stale and repetitive to him. I can hear it in his voice, see it in his eyes. He begins to say no to our afternoon times more regularly, until I find myself pleading with him, "Connor, I need to see you, I need us to be together." But even when we're together it's not the same anymore. Increasingly he just lays there passively allowing me to do whatever I wish to do, but seemingly disconnecting himself from me, from us. He rarely makes eye contact. When he comes he makes hardly any sound at all, just a little grunt. He doesn't want to talk afterwards. He doesn't want to shower together. He doesn't want me to touch him at all, really. I'm as unwanted as an old strip of film on a cutting room floor.

***

He's taken off his sneakers and socks and pants and is standing in the middle of the room in his shirt and shorts when, facing away from me, he says, "I don't want to do this anymore."

"C'mere, Connor," I say, patting the bed. I've been ready for him for several minutes.

"I mean it."

"Come over here and tell me all about it."

"No." He turns around, faces me. "If I do you'll just…just *grab* me and I'll get—confused."

"You mean horny?"

He makes a disgusted face. "You shouldn't say things like that."

"If you come over here we don't have to talk at all."

He stands disconsolately, looking down. "Mona, I don't want to do this anymore. You said we could stop if I wanted to. I want to stop."

"Aren't you having fun?"

"Not really."

"We can do anything you want, Connor. Together. Anything at all."

"I don't *want* to do—nasty things with you. I feel like I want to take a bath after we do things."

"I'll take a bath with you, sweetie."

"That's not what I mean." He turns, pushes the curtains aside a few inches and looks out to the street. "Sometimes I think I just want to kill myself."

I sit up. "Honey, no."

He speaks very quietly, very sadly. "I feel like a—like a *fake* with Kylie. I feel like some kind of pervert. Like a sex maniac."

"You're not doing anything with her, though, are you?"

"No. That's just it. It's like—like I'm the man who knew too much." He scoffs sadly at his own Hitchcock metaphor. "She doesn't know anything. I don't think she knows where babies come from."

"Well, maybe you're just too mature for her, sweetheart."

"I'm *not*, though. I really *like* her. She's funny. You don't hear it 'cuz she's shy around other people but she's really funny. The things she says about people. The, like, the things she notices. She makes me laugh. It's just that I feel like she's a little girl and I'm…I don't know." He seems to consider. "If we'd never started all this stuff I wouldn't feel this way. I wouldn't know any more than she does. Or—at least not that much more. We'd be like—like *the same age*. I…I don't know. It's just weird." He falls silent.

"I'm sorry, Connor," I say at last, sincerely.

He doesn't respond.

"But you have me, you know, sweetheart. And I love you."

He looks back at me, his expression unreadable. "Yeah," he says in a flat voice. "I have you."

***

But I don't have him, not anymore. There's a terrible dropping sensation in my heart, a sick feeling of vertigo, as if my stomach were coming up through my throat. It's over, it's ending, it's finished, it's done. He doesn't want me anymore. I get up that afternoon from bed and put my clothes on and Connor puts on his and we drive in silence back to the city, time wasted, money wasted, risk wasted. During the drive I start to cry and to my amazement I find I can't stop. I hold both hands tight on the steering wheel and cry. The tears run down my face and onto my blouse. Some drip onto my skirt. My throat is so tight I can hardly breathe. I try to stay quiet because I suspect Connor will get angry with me. I don't shriek, I don't wail. I just cry, cry silently, cry, cry. Connor doesn't respond. He doesn't even look at me.

***

But it's not over, not really. I see him every day, after all, in class. I call on him and help him and grade his work. Our eyes meet, filled with things that can't be spoken. Every day at lunchtime Connor reads with Kylie outside and laughs with her and on Saturdays he visits her with her mom present—Kylie tells me this—but he knows, I know he knows, that there's an emptiness to it, a childishness. He can't get from her what he gets from me. And so I'm not really that surprised when, a few weeks later, Connor sheepishly approaches me at my desk when the other students have stepped out and asks quietly, "Mona, could we go to a motel later?"

"I thought you wanted to end it, Connor. That's what you told me."

"I know, I—but I didn't mean forever."

"I thought you did."

"I just meant—I don't want to do it so much anymore. So often."

"*Is* that what you meant, Connor?"

He stands nervously, hands in his pockets, moving restlessly from foot to foot. I can see the bulge in his jeans. "Please, Mona?"

I study him, feel the power in the relationship surging back to me. "Sure, Connor. We can go."

***

And for an hour or two it's as it was, reanimated, rekindled, we're wild with each other in bed, laughing and squealing and tickling each other and the bed banging against the wall and making love again and again. I'm amazed anew at his resilience, his incredible physical intensity. I can tell from his eyes, wide, rolling back in his head as he comes, that he's amazed with me, with what we do, a universe away from the milk and cookies and cartoons he shares with Kylie McCloud. For this one time there's no friction, no disappointment, no boredom, there's just Connor and me as we once were, ravished, ravishing, passionate, loving, in love.

***

And yet the next day he's short with me, seemingly annoyed, he doesn't make eye contact, he spends all his time with Kylie and ignores me completely in class except when I actually call on him. Even then he looks away, says, "I don't know, Ms. Straw, I forgot to study," and returns to his silence. For days he acts as if I'm his worst teacher, as if he can't stand my class and is just going through the motions of reading and writing because he has to. I have to repeatedly shush him from talking to Kylie. But I sense that some of this is a performance on Connor's part. I've never had trouble with him in class, not even when he became friends with Kylie. He's a polite, well-mannered boy. He knows how to behave in my class. He's doing it on purpose, I realize. He's showing me how much she means to him, how little I do.

But after what happened the other day I know it won't last, and it doesn't. A week or two later he approaches me again, sheepish expression on his face, bulge in his pants.

"Can we, Mona?"

I frown. "You haven't been very nice to me, Connor."

"I'm sorry. But can we?"

The truth is that I can't resist him any more than he can me, and he knows it. But I say, "Connor, I'm not a service station, you know. To just be there whenever you need a fill up. I'm a person. I have feelings."

"I said I was sorry. Can we?"

And of course we do. But this time I know what he meant before, about feeling dirty. I've never felt that way with Connor, but this time I do. He hardly talks, just starts taking off his clothes the second the motel room door is shut, strokes his erection. "C'mon, Mona, hurry up," he says, scowling at me. I obediently take off my things. He doesn't smile. He doesn't say *Wow* or *Oh my God* or tell me how beautiful I am.

Instead he says: "I want you to suck my dick."

I flush with embarrassment. "Connor!"

"Please," he adds, his tone unmistakably sarcastic.

"Don't talk to me like that."

"Like what? I *said* please."

"Don't use words like that. That kind of language."

"You mean 'suck my dick'?"

"Yes."

He scoffs. "You've done it before. Lots of times."

"Connor—that's not how to talk about that stuff. With your girlfriend. Your lover. It's disrespectful."

"What do you know about respect?"

This feels wrong, terribly wrong, the two of us standing in this room that smells of roach spray looking at each other's nakedness and arguing. I find myself sitting down, crossing my legs, folding my arms over my breasts. But I don't move to put my clothes on.

"Connor," I say, holding my voice as steady as I can, "you have to be nice to someone who's nice to you. Who makes you feel good. You shouldn't make her feel bad."

"Do you have feelings, Mona?"

"I—what does that mean?"

He shrugs. "I don't know. I just want you to suck my dick. I've been thinking about it all day."

"If you want me to do that then you need to be nice to me."

"I think I'm pretty nice. I haven't told the principal or my dad yet. I haven't called the police."

"What do you mean, 'yet'?"

He shrugs again.

"Connor, we've talked about all this before. *You* ended our relationship and then *you* started it up again. I didn't, you did. You love me, even if you don't want to admit it."

"So?"

"So would you talk to Kylie this way? Would you demand something instead of asking politely for it...?"

"I wouldn't ask her for *this.*"

"Not *this.* Just something. Would you demand that she kiss you on the cheek at the same time you told her that she didn't have feelings and wasn't respectful and threatened to call the police on her?"

"I didn't threaten."

"Yes, you did."

"I just want you to suck on it, that's all."

He stands there, eyes cold. Finally I unfold my arms, my legs, I slink to my knees on the dirty carpet. He doesn't touch me. Doesn't smooth my hair, doesn't reach down to stroke my cheek, doesn't say how good it feels. He just stands there with his hands on his hips looking—*glaring*—down at me. I notice the little blonde pubic hairs starting to sprout from his skin. After a while he comes quietly, dispassionately. I fight back revulsion, the sudden impulse to spit it all out on the motel room carpet. I swallow. It makes my throat dry. I want a glass of water but I just stay there on my knees, not meeting Connor's awful look, embarrassed, humiliated for the first time, the very first time with him. Then he delivers the hammer blow.

He says, "You're a slut."

He turns and begins putting on his clothes again. I don't move, don't breathe. All I want to do at this exact moment in time is die, just die. I think: *Die. Die now.* I try to kill myself using my mind, force my heart to slow and stop. *Die. Die.*

But I don't die, and in a minute Connor says impatiently, "C'mon, put your clothes on. I want to go home."

19

My dreams are strange, uneasy, unearthly. I'm in an empty house calling for my parents, I'm a little girl, calling and calling but no one answers. I'm with Connor in a motel room and I'm covered with bruises, he's hitting me, slapping me in the face, pulling me by the hair and shoving my head into the toilet and calling me a slut. Gracie stands there watching, saying nothing, drinking from her sippy cup. Bill's there too, behind her, dressed in his old hippie gear, shaking his head. I'm on a moor somewhere, mud, craggy cliffs, it's windy, rain in the air, Connor is with me, we're handcuffed tightly together, my wrist is chafed, bleeding, something is chasing us in the glowering dark and I'm telling him that we can get out of this if we stick together but he's pulling away, trying to get out of the cuffs, trying to run from me. I'm in front of a mirror, I'm twelve years old and there's only half of me, I'm standing on one leg, I have only one arm, half my head, one eye, a half-set of lips, I realize suddenly I'll never be any different than this, I'm trapped in this body, this half-body, and I try to scream but my half-mouth doesn't work, it won't open, I don't even have that escape, that release. I'm at school, in front of the class talking about verb tenses and I'm dressed soberly and professionally but they're naked, all of them, Lauren Holloway and Richard Broad and Kevin Simmons and Douglas Peterson and Cheryl Minton and Andrew Harrington and Kylie and Connor and all the rest and I look at their pale little undeveloped bodies in embarrassment, ask them why they're naked and tell them to put on their clothes and Kylie says, *We can't, Ms. Straw, you took our clothes.*

***

Quiet evenings. Normal evenings. Pick up Gracie, do the shopping, come home, make dinner, watch TV, read, play children's games, put my daughter to bed, grow sleepy. Let Bill make love to me if he wants, but he's as tired as I am, usually he doesn't. Then sleep. Simple. The way millions of other people live. Nothing complicated, nothing difficult. Countless people do it successfully every day. Just life, that's all. Except that I'm not really there, I'm an automaton, a zombie, my heart has stopped, it's gone from my chest entirely. I perform my role as an actor would a part in a long-running play, smoothly, competently, a bit of my mind somewhere else while sheer technique and professionalism take over and carry me through from scene to scene. It doesn't matter where my heart is or my brain as long as I deliver my lines convincingly, as long as I stand in the right place at the right time and do what I'm supposed to do. The play goes on then, with well-meshed gears. Ms. Straw, Mona Straw is where she's supposed to be, doing what she's supposed to do. And so everything is all right.

***

Once I find myself with some spare time—an almost unheard-of occurrence. I have no grading to do, I'm not kept late at school, no shopping needs to be done, Gracie doesn't have to be picked up for over an hour. I'm tempted to go home and take a nap but instead I drive to the mall, something I never do unless I'm with Bill and Gracie. I treat myself to a soft-serve ice cream cone with multi-colored sprinkles and wander around for a while, look at clothes, jewelry, just window shopping. I find myself passing by the racy lingerie shop and on impulse I step into it, not looking for anything in particular, just whiling away time. To my surprise I discover it's not just lingerie, sexy black bras and V-cut panties and such. In the rear of the store is all manner of sexual paraphernalia, some of it quite shocking to see in this family-friendly mall. Dildos, leather things, whips, hardcore porn videos. I'd had no idea. A clerk, a pretty red-haired woman younger than I, steps up and asks if she can help me. I'm so embarrassed I nearly drop my ice cream cone, nearly flee the shop entirely, but manage to smile and say, "No thanks, I'm just looking."

As she smiles and turns away I notice something on a corner table: a set of little pink fuzzy handcuffs. I pick them up curiously, assuming they're just a toy—they're sort of cute, certainly not big and imposing like the merciless silver steel ones the police carry with them. These seem only half that size. But they're real. They're made of metal, some kind of metal that's been covered over with the sort of fluffy material familiar to me from Gracie's stuffed animals. But despite the softness of the covering the two cuffs are hard, unforgiving. A short chain connects them, also metal, I think steel, which seems to have been sprayed over with gold paint. Like the cuffs themselves the chain is also not terribly large, but it's surprisingly strong. I finish my ice cream cone to free my hand and then pull at the cuffs experimentally, first gently, then with more force. They don't give. These are actual handcuffs. On one cuff is a small bit of folded blue cardboard dangling from a string. I unfold it and see two little gold keys wrapped in plastic along with a note printed in poor English: *THESE ARE REAL DEVICE! USE AT OWN RISK! DO NOT LOOSE KEYS!*

I stand there for a long time looking at the little pink handcuffs. I see how they can be adjusted for different sized wrists. I pull at them again and again, to determine if I can break the chain. I look around to see if the clerk is watching me but she's busy with another customer. Anyway, if I break them it doesn't matter, I'll just buy them and throw them in the trash bin outside the store. I pull, pull again. They don't break. I'm not strong enough to break them. Something shocks me that these can even be sold openly in a store in a mall, but there's nothing illegal, I suppose, in buying handcuffs or owning them. These are obviously designed for sex games, bondage games, perfectly innocent fantasy play for adults with otherwise boring middle-class lives.

I look around the shop, empty but for the red-haired clerk and her single other customer. My scalp is tingling, sweat is running down my neck. On the back of the bit of folded cardboard the price is marked. I'm astounded at how high it is, but this isn't a cheap plastic toy. I know I have enough cash in my purse—I would never consider putting this purchase on

Visa for Bill to read about later even if it weren't itemized, even if only the name of the store appeared on the bill. I look out the front window of the shop to the mall beyond, wondering if anyone I know could possibly be lurking around, any teacher, any friend, any student's parent. Ms. Straw being seen in the shop would be bad enough, but Ms. Straw buying pink handcuffs?

I buy the handcuffs.

The clerk doesn't bat an eye, just drops them into a paper sack, hands me my change and receipt, says brightly, "Thank you, come again!" I smile, stuff the sack into my purse, rush from the shop down the escalator and to my car. As soon as I'm inside with the door locked I take a quick glance around the parking lot to make sure no one is near and then take the cuffs from the bag, rip the keys from their plastic wrapper. I close first one cuff—it gives a satisfying *snap*—and open it with one of the keys. Then I close the other and open it. It sticks just slightly, but then works fine. But to be sure, to be confident in both the locks and the keys, I encircle my own wrist with a cuff, tighten it, snap it shut. I'm breathing heavily, as if I've been running a marathon. How would I explain a pink fuzzy handcuff stuck on my wrist to the sales clerk, to anyone? But when I insert the key and turn it the device works perfectly, the cuff pops open. The same thing happens with the other cuff. No problem at all. I loop one of the little keys onto my regular key ring, leave the other at the bottom of my purse. I push the handcuffs themselves into an inner side pocket—I'll hide them later, I think, somewhere at home. There is a garbage container near the car and I get out, crumple up the bag and receipt and throw them away. I return to the car again, shut the door, lock it.

I close my eyes then, rest my head against the back of the seat, try to breathe. I think of Connor pouring over the book of Hitchcock's films, think of him looking at the picture of Robert Donat and Madeleine Carroll handcuffed together on the moor, think of how close our hands were then, how I nearly reached out and encircled his hand with my own, how we both gazed at the photo and how he said that he wanted to see that movie.

***

Dear Ms. Straw,

I am very sorry I called you that word. It was very rude of me. I am sorry I hurt your feelings. I hope we can be friends again. Like we were before.

Sincerly,
Connor Blue. (Your student.)

***

Another motel room, the last motel room. He says, "I love you, Mona," he makes love to me, it's the way it was, but afterward he turns away as if he's ashamed of himself, or of me, or of us together. He withdraws into silence again.

After a while he suddenly asks, in a remote, indifferent voice, "Mona, how long do child molesters go to jail for?"

***

He spends his days with Kylie. He doesn't speak to me.

***

Dominoes falling. Looking through my box in the faculty room at school I find another mailing from Youth Leadership for America, a reminder about their annual conference happening in just a few weeks and telling me that there's still time to register up to two students for this "wonderful opportunity," a day-long conference tailored to fifth- through eighth-graders about "leadership, community, and caring." The young co-star of a current teen sitcom will make an appearance, a Maryland state senator will speak, students will brainstorm ideas about building community, create a group art project on the theme, have fun, think, learn. Lots of food, competitions, door prizes. Hundreds are expected to attend.

The price is low, and the school is willing to foot the bill if I want to take my Saturday to drive a couple of students up to Harrisburg for the event. I've done it with kids once or twice before. Parents must be talked to, of course, permission forms have to be signed. It will wipe out my Saturday, from early morning to night. Bill will have to take care of Gracie. And yet dominoes are falling in my mind, I can feel them. Gears meshing, slipping into place.

***

I don't ask them separately, I ask them together at the end of a Friday after-school session. I request that Connor and Kylie stay behind for a moment and they do. I show them the brochure, talk up the event, tell them what an exciting opportunity it is.

"I can register up to two students," I say. "I thought you two might enjoy it."

Connor and I exchange a look. "Why us?"

"Because I think you're a natural leader," I say to him. "And Kylie, you're coming out of your shell so much now. I think this would be really good for you." Her smile is big, as it always is when she receives the kind of positive attention from me or anyone that she's not yet used to. "It would be fun, anyway. Something different to do. Just the three of us, together for the day."

"I want to go!" Kylie says. Her excitement is obvious. Kylie is not a girl accustomed to being picked for anything.

Connor is more reserved about it, but he's intrigued. He obviously understands that this is an overture on my part, a peace offering, my way of telling him that it's all right, he and I can be friends, friends and nothing more, I can support him as a teacher should and in no other way.

"I can talk to your dad about it, Connor, if you want me to," I say.

He shrugs, hands the brochure back to me. "Sure. I mean, it's okay. I'll go. If Kylie wants to."

"Fantastic!" I say, grinning at them both. "We'll have a great day, I promise. I'll talk to your dad, Connor, and Kylie, I'll call your mom about it. Here's the permission forms, okay? Get them signed and bring them back as soon as you can."

***

The phone conversations with the parents are brief and simple. Connor's dad just says fine, he'll sign it. Kylie's mom is more curious, unaccustomed to having her daughter singled out for something like this. I tell her about the conference, talk up how well Kylie has been doing, emphasize that I'll be chaperoning them every minute. Finally she says yes and thanks me. The permission forms come back from both kids the next day, signed.

20

The Saturday arrives with dark gray clouds approaching in the sky and a forecast for rain. Bill kisses me at the door and wishes me a good conference. Gracie hugs me. That's the hardest moment, Gracie's little arms around my leg. I pick her up for a moment, press her face against my neck, tell her how much I love her, that I'll never stop loving her. "You be a good girl for Daddy, okay?"

"I will."

I smile, put her down again, wipe my eyes.

"Hey," Bill says, "what's up? Why the tears?"

"Just allergies," I say. I kiss him on the cheek. "Take care of Gracie, Bill."

"I will. We're going to the movies later." He picks her up.

"That's great. That's great." I try to keep my voice steady. "I trust you, Bill. I know you'll always be a good dad to her."

"Hm?"

"Take care of her, okay?"

"You bet," he says, smiling but with a slightly puzzled expression on his face.

I toss my bag into the car, start the motor, sit there for a moment looking at my husband with our daughter in his arms, these two people who love me and whom I'll never see again. I back out of the driveway quickly, not wanting to burst completely into tears that can't be explained away by unreal allergies. My nerves are jumping under my skin. I'm sweating although it's cool in the car. As I stop to shift the vehicle into drive I check my purse and make sure it's securely closed. The handcuffs are in the purse, and Bill's gun.

***

There's time to change my mind, of course. There's time to turn back, to tell Bill I've suddenly taken sick, to provide evidence by sticking my finger down my throat in the bathroom and retching my breakfast, to have him call Connor and Kylie's parents and explain that his wife is very ill, she's terribly sorry but she's not going to be able to take the kids to the conference after all. It would all end then. After I convinced Bill that it just seems to be indigestion or food poisoning and that the worst of it appears to have passed, that what I need now is sleep, he would go ahead and take Gracie to the movies and I would bury the handcuffs in a box or bag or something and stuff it down deep into our garbage can outside and then replace Bill's gun in the drawer and there would be nothing, absolutely nothing that had happened except a couple of mildly disappointed kids who would no doubt get together at Kylie's house that day anyway for snacks and TV. On Monday I'd apologize profusely to them, say we'll be sure to go next year, even if I knew we wouldn't. I could get another teacher to take them, maybe. Anyway it wouldn't matter. It would be over, the crisis passed, life would return to normal.

But it can't do that, I know. *Normal* is not an option anymore, hasn't been for many months, almost the entire school year. Maybe my entire life. *Normal* is something other people are, not me. I have no choice in what I'm about to do, not really. I've had no choice for a long time.

***

The drive to Harrisburg is a quietly excited one. They sit together in the back, Connor occasionally asking a question, Kylie looking out the window in between bouts of reading her latest big fantasy novel. I've made sure she has her asthma inhaler with her. I can see Connor in my rear view mirror; we make eye contact a few times. I smile, say friendly teacher things. Traffic is light and we make good time. Once Kylie asks that we stop because she has to go to the bathroom. We do. She comes out again while Connor is in the men's room and she scampers quickly up to me, book in hand, tugs on my sleeve.

"Ms. Straw?"

"Yes, Kylie?"

"Do you think I shouldn't read my book on the trip?"

"Well, I don't know. I guess that's up to you."

"'Cuz my mom says I shouldn't. She says it's rude. But I was at a really good part."

"I'm sure Connor would like it if you talked to him a little, Kylie, instead of reading. But whatever you're comfortable with."

"Okay," she says. "I'll stop."

And she does, she becomes part of the conversation as we continue the drive on this ever-darkening Saturday morning. Looking in my mirror I notice at one point that they're holding hands and looking away from each other, out their own car windows. Finally we're there, only a little late. It's a long day, but fun because they find it fun. In truth much of this conference is more like a carnival than anything really educational, but there are some presentations, some interactive workshops, a few short speeches. Kylie gets very excited at seeing the TV actor, who she recognizes. Maybe two hundred kids and grown-ups are there in the auditorium. Connor and Kylie become part of a small group of kids who paint a big rough mural on the theme of "community." They brainstorm ideas on how to bring people from different backgrounds together. They listen to the state senator talk about the political process and why kids should learn about it now. They eat lots of pizza and drink lots of soda. This is all pretty much as it's been in previous years.

Even now, I know, I could change my mind. When the festivities conclude I could simply hustle the kids into the car, remind them to put on their seat belts, and drive back home. Ms. Straw would get yet more points for being a wonderful, committed teacher, taking her entire Saturday to drive two kids to a youth leadership conference, to stay with them all day, to drive them back home in the evening, all for no extra pay. Mrs. McCloud would be delighted to see her daughter come home so happy, finally a chosen one, a special student who has received special attention. Mr. Blue wouldn't care, of course, but maybe the day would at least calm things down between Connor and me, show him that I care about him whether or not we're together. Really together.

But none of those things will happen because in my purse I have the handcuffs and the gun. I haven't even completely articulated within my own mind exactly what I'm going to do with them. I only know that we're not going home.

Finally the day ends with colored lights and music and cheers and *Thanks for coming, we'll see you next year* and hundreds of kids and adults pouring out into the parking lot. Car doors slam, engines start. We don't move at all for quite some time. My nerves start to jump again, the steering wheel grows moist with sweat. When we finally get to the exit I see the sign for the freeway south, which is the direction of home. I take the exit north.

***

"Are we lost?" Connor asks, a long time later, the sun dim and low in the steely sky.

"Just taking a different route," I say confidently. "Such nice scenery, don't you think?" And there is a great deal of greenery around us. I'm surprised at how well I remember the route to the cabin, considering that Bill always drove and I've not been there in years.

***

Darkness. Headlights on the narrow country road.

"We are *definitely* lost," Connor says.

"Are we lost, Ms. Straw?" asks Kylie, her tone not unhappy.

"Only a little bit," I say. "I know where we are. I just need to find the main road. We'll be home in just a little while."

***

It's farther than I remembered. By now they both know that something is wrong—not with Ms. Straw, but with our location.

"Mona, do you have a map?" Connor asks. "I'll try to figure out where we are. I'm pretty good with maps." He turns to Kylie. "Why are you laughing?"

"You called Ms. Straw 'Mona'!"

"Oh, yeah." He smiles a little. "Sorry, Ms. Straw."

***

"Maybe we should stop, kids," I say as we near the cabin. "I'll check to see if there's a map in the trunk. Maybe we can find somebody to ask. I'm awfully sorry about this."

They're surprisingly calm about it. I realize that their faith in Ms. Straw's ability to take care of things is absolute—even Connor's faith. It strikes me that for him *Ms. Straw* and *Mona* must really be two essentially different people. The one he knows as Ms. Straw is smoothly professional and competent at all times, and thanks to Kylie's presence it's Ms. Straw he's with now, or thinks that he is. The teacher, the authority figure, the one who runs things. For him *Mona* must seem far away.

At last we pull up to the cabin in the darkness. My headlights shine on it through the rain that's begun to fall: the structure seems in decent repair, though it's a bit dilapidated, the roof sagging in spots. I hope the locks haven't rusted, that I can get in without difficulty.

"Where are we?" Connor asks.

"You know what?" I say brightly. "I realized a little ways back that I recognized this road. I actually know where we are. My husband and I own this cabin."

Connor looks strangely at me. "Really?"

"Wow!" Kylie says. "That's cool! You own a cabin in the woods!"

"Yeah," I smile. "Want to take a look? Now that I'm sure where we are, getting home will be a cinch." I pull the car under the canopy, the closest thing we have to a garage here, shut off the motor. "Still, Connor, I'm pretty sure I have a map in the trunk. We'll look. Let's make sure I don't make any boo-boos on the way back."

"Boo-boos!" Kylie giggles, looking at me with her head tilted back. "Ms. Straw, I have to go to the bathroom again."

"Okay. Let's go in." We step out. The rain is falling hard now, making a racket on the canopy. I fumble with my bag, drop the keys on the ground, pick them up. It's very dark. I unlock the trunk, pull it open. Jumper cables, old boxes, general detritus. "Connor, have a look around in the junk here, will you? For a map? I'll turn on the light for you. Come on, Kylie." I find the front door lock, insert the key, open the door.

The cabin smells musty, of course. I switch on the porch light and a light in the living room.

"Neat," Kylie says. "But I thought it would look more like a log cabin. Like Abe Lincoln's house."

I smile. "I know, this is really just a regular house, isn't it? Only smaller." My heartbeat is pounding behind my eyes. The rain falls, falls. "The bathroom's in here, Kylie." I lead her to it, open the door for her, turn on the light. "The lock doesn't work," I lie. "But I'll stand here and make sure Connor doesn't come in."

"Thanks, Ms. Straw."

She closes the door. I stand there for what feels like centuries. Connor is still out at the car; I can see the hood of the trunk sticking up from here. My breath is shallow. I feel dizzy. I can back out, I think. I can stop. I can put them in the car even now and go home, tell a whopper of a story to Bill and their parents about getting hopelessly confused on the freeway, driving in the wrong direction without realizing it, not understanding until I recognized that we were fairly near our cabin, deciding to go there to give the kids a bathroom break and me a driving break before returning home at last. I can do that, I think. I can do that. The bag drops from my hands, sags on the floor. I've been standing here for centuries and yet Connor hasn't come in, I haven't heard a thing from Kylie in the bathroom. Centuries. Sweat pours down my face although it's cool in the room, cool and musty. I find myself wondering ridiculously if there's any food in the cupboards, if I could offer them anything to eat. But no. Hurry up please it's time.

I turn, step into the bathroom, lock the door behind me. Kylie is standing at the toilet, having just pulled down her pants. They're around her ankles, the jeans and the little white panties with red hearts she has on under them. I've caught her in the moment before she sits down. She looks at me with such astonishment that she doesn't make a sound, doesn't act embarrassed or cry out, "Ms. Straw!" or cover her privates with her hands or anything. She just looks at me through her glasses, head tilted back, mouth open. For a moment I realize why people generally dislike her, she looks so stupid standing there like that, she looks like a two-legged cow, like a brainless doll with nothing but white plastic between her legs, no hair at all. In the instant I move toward her she suddenly realizes that something is very wrong and tries to turn away from me but her pants tangle up her feet. She nearly falls but I catch her from behind, pull her head back, tighten my hands around her throat. "Shh, shh," I say, my voice ragged and strange, "don't make a sound, Kylie, shh." I squeeze as hard as I can. The only sound she makes is a little gurgling noise. Her hands fly this way and that, like they did the moment Connor started the slow dance with her. She tries to reach me behind her but can only flail backwards at my shoulders and thighs. But I can't get enough pressure on her neck, it's almost impossible this way. I'm choking her but she's managing little breaths. She tries to wrench loose, weak little girl, stumbles over her pants, nearly drags both of us down, I lose my balance, too much of her weight is in my hands and suddenly we're on our knees, I'm on top of her from behind, my hands are on fire with the pain of the squeezing and yet she's not dying, she's kicking and pulling at my fingers and managing quick gasping breaths and I suddenly know that this isn't going to work, she's stronger than I realized, I should never have tried from behind, I use all my strength to force her down flat on the floor, implant my knee on her back, take my hands off her throat, she inhales hugely with an odd high-pitched sound like wind whistling in a canyon, I grab her mousy hair in my hands and slam her face onto the bathroom tile as hard as I can. Twice, three times. Suddenly I realize I'm wet, my pants are wet, my leg pushed against her back and bottom, she's peeing herself, great waves of piss pouring out from between her legs and somehow this makes me angry, makes me slam her head against the tile harder, harder still, ten times, twenty, until finally her body seems to shiver hugely and her fluttering arms drop to the floor, make only weak spasmodic motions. Incredibly, piss is still coming out of her. I turn her over, both of us covered in urine. Her eyes are rolled up in her head and her face is covered with blood: her nose is smashed, I realize, pouring sticky red tendrils everywhere across her face. Her forehead is covered with ugly raw abrasions. One of her front teeth is split nearly in half. Yet the thing I notice the most, more vividly than anything else, is how odd she looks without her glasses on. They've flown off her face and landed I don't know where. But as I lean down to her I realize she's not dead. Her breathing is ragged, shaky, she's moaning. She's not dead. Connor's voice suddenly, so close that for an instant I think he's come into the room: "Where are you guys? Kylie? Ms. Straw?" With his voice I begin again to hear the rain, in mad torrent now, a deluge slamming down on the cabin, surely we'll all be swept away. I wrap my hands around her neck again, this time from the front, and press down. Her face turns red, then blue, then an odd, sick gray. My fingers ache but now my thumbs can completely crush the soft part of her throat, press, press, a small high-pitched sound like a trapped rat comes from her and then I feel something collapse in her throat, my thumbs push through something, her body bucks for a second or two, her arms twitch, and she's dead. I know it the instant it happens. She's dead.

I lean back, breathing heavily, looking down at this stranger, this little person who is a stranger to me. The room smells of piss. I'm soaked with my sweat and her pee. I move aside, look away from her as Connor knocks on the bathroom door. "Is one of you in there? Kylie? Mona?"

You called Ms. Straw 'Mona'!

I feel too weak to stand. I drag myself to the bathroom door, unlock it. After a moment Connor turns the knob and pokes his head in. "What...?"

I drag myself to the wall, lean my back against it, close my eyes, try to catch my breath. For a moment I don't know what he does, how he looks. Then I hear a high-pitched wailing sound and for a moment I think she's come back to life, I haven't killed her, I haven't set Connor and me free. He pushes through the door, I open my eyes, he steps in and immediately his feet fly out in front of him and he crashes down, a classic Buster Keaton pratfall, right on his bottom on the piss-slick floor. He doesn't seem to notice me. He stares at Kylie, his eyes saucer-round, his mouth open as hers so often was. The high-pitched sound comes from him again, wavering, not loud. We don't move for a moment. Then Connor stands, his pants wet now, backs out into the bathroom doorway. Finally he looks at me. I wait for him to say something but he doesn't, just makes the sound, backs away a little further until he's out of the bathroom entirely. He's wringing his hands, literally pacing and wringing his hands like some old woman in a Russian novel. Finally I manage to stand. I splash water on my face, drink a few handfuls, then step out to face Connor.

"We need to make some decisions now," I say.

He looks at me as if I'm the vilest creature on the planet, something unclean, beyond redemption. I wish he'd close his mouth. I wish he'd stop pacing. He looks silly.

"Connor, there are some things we'll need to do now," I say.

He covers his face with his hands for a moment, realizes they're covered with urine, wipes them on his pants, turns away from me, turns back again.

"I need you to be a man now, Connor."

His wail begins to form into words. The first word is "I." It takes him a moment to get out the rest. Finally he screams: "I—I—I—*I hate you!*"

This sets loose a flood of tears as he paces, paces, slaps meaninglessly at the walls, turns again to the bathroom and then quickly away.

I move to him, wrap my arms around him. "Cry it out, sweetheart. I know this is hard for you."

"Get away from me!" He backs up, eyes wild. "You're— you're *crazy!*"

"I know you're upset, sweetheart."

"Don't call me 'sweetheart'!"

"Try to calm down, Connor. If you think about it you'll know why I had to do it."

He covers his ears, just like a little boy, grits his teeth, turns away. Then he turns to the bathroom again, looks in, as if to convince himself that it's real. I take that moment to grab his arm, turn him to me.

"Connor, we have things we have to do now."

"I'm not doing anything with you."

"We need to take care of this."

"Take care of *what?*"

I gesture. "That."

His expression is perplexed, exasperated. "What are you talking about?"

"We can't just leave Kylie lying there in the bathroom, Connor."

He rips away from me, his expression suddenly fierce. "I'm going to call the police." He looks around. "Where's the phone?"

"We don't have one here, baby."

He looks toward my bag. "You must have a cell phone."

I take the bag up in my hands hurriedly. "I don't."

"I don't believe you."

"I've never lied to you, Connor." Oddly enough, I *don't* have a cell phone.

"Let me see. Let me look in your bag."

"Connor, we have more important things to worry about now. We have to deal with—" I gesture again.

"I'm not dealing with anything. I'm getting out of here." He moves toward the door.

"Do you have any idea where you are, sweetheart?"

"No. But I'll find somebody. In another cabin. Or I'll get back down to the main road."

"In this downpour? With no light? I think you'll find that difficult."

"I don't care!"

"You're going to stay here with me, Connor. You're going to stay here with me and help me clean up this mess, just like the responsible young man you are."

"Why should I help you?"

"Because you're my accomplice, sweetheart."

"Me? You did it!"

"With your help. That's her pee all over you, Connor."

"I didn't do it!"

"The police might think that you did. That you helped me."

"Why would I do it?"

"Because you wanted it to be just you and me," I say. "The same thing I want."

"That's crazy!"

"They'll have a lot of evidence against you, sweetheart."

He shakes his head. "I'm leaving."

I had hoped it wouldn't come to this, but so be it. I pull the gun from the bag, aim it at him.

"Connor, you're going to help me."

Oddly, he doesn't look particularly shocked. Perhaps his face's capacity for expressing emotion has reached its limit. He just scowls at me.

"We're going to take care of it, Connor. You and me."

"How?" he says at last, watching me, watching the gun.

"We have some tools at the back of the house. There's a shovel. We're going to dig a hole and put her in it."

He looks at me for a long time. Then he seems to suddenly deflate. He drops onto the sofa and cries. I move to him, sit next to him.

"Connor," I say, "I need you to be a man now. I don't need a little boy. I need a man."

"But I'm *not* a man," he says at last, his voice tight.

"Yes, you are. After what we've done together? You're a man, sweetheart. And I need you to act like one. I need your help. Mona needs your help."

"I hate you," he says again, quietly.

I stand again, gun at my side. "Come on, Connor," I say firmly. "I'll show you the tools."

***

The rain becomes a storm. Lightning, thunder, torrential downpours in the dark. We work from the weak glow of the rear porch lamp and a couple of flashlights. I choose a spot some thirty yards from the back of the house, easy to cover with shrubbery once we're done. No one ever comes here. No one will know. For a while I stand watching him dig with the gun at my side but after a while I see that he's accepted that he's part of this, part of me, I needn't threaten him anymore. I put the gun in my bag and keep the bag over my shoulder. He digs for a while, and then I do. We switch again and again. It's backbreaking work. I thought with all the rain it would be relatively easy, but mud is heavy. After an hour we finish a hole maybe three feet deep.

"That's enough," I say at last. "Go get her, Connor."

He's panting, his face covered in rain. "Me? I can't."

"I need you to."

"I *can't*, Mona!"

"Oh, *Connor.*" I move, every muscle crying out in pain, toward the house, bag over my shoulder. It doesn't cross my mind that Connor might run while I'm gone. He's part of this now. He knows he is. In the house I step in, tracking mud everywhere, move to the bathroom, take her by both feet and pull. I can hardly believe how heavy this little girl is. I drag her to the rear of the house, her hands up above her head now, as if she were surrendering to the police in an old film noir. I push backwards through the screen door at the back, step into the rain again, drag her out toward the grave.

Connor cries out suddenly, "Mona! Oh my God!"

"What?"

"Pull up her pants! Pull up her pants, Mona! Oh my God!"

"It doesn't matter now," I say, looking at her mud-spattered knees and thighs and privates.

"Please, Mona!"

I can see he's going to become hysterical, so I lean down and do what I can. It's almost impossible with a dead body, mud, darkness, rain. A few feet away I can hear Connor vomiting in the bushes.

"There," I say, standing again. "I did it. Now come on."

He follows as I drag Kylie to the edge of the muddy hole, pull her partway into it, step around the side to pull her farther along by her arms. Finally she's in place.

"Get her things from the car, Connor."

He doesn't protest this. While he's gone I move to the bathroom again, look for evidence of her presence. I find none other than the urine everywhere, which we'll clean before we go.

He returns with Kylie's things in her little rucksack, a pitiful collection of relics: Kleenex, asthma inhaler, a notebook with unicorns on the cover, pen, pencil stub, gum wrappers, and, of course, a thick fantasy novel. I leave it all in the bag and push the bag down beside her. I can hardly see in this rain, this interminable rain.

"Is that everything?"

He nods. He's crying.

"Then take the shovel, Connor."

"Wait," he says weakly.

"We don't have time to wait."

"Wait."

He steps to the edge of the grave, looks down at the dead girl. Mud is all over her, her body, her shirt, her ruined red-splashed face. Her hair is askew. I can see that he's thinking of trying to tidy her up. He moves from one side of the grave to the other, running his hands through his drenched hair. At last he steps near her head and takes something from his pocket, crouches down to her.

It's her glasses. He places them gently onto her pulpy nose and over her ears and then turns away weeping, still crouched, mud covering his pants.

I take the shovel myself and finish the task.

***

After that Connor is all but useless. He sits on the sofa, arms wrapped around himself, shivering. His eyes are wide, staring at nothing in particular. His breathing seems erratic. He makes little gasping sounds. Sometimes his breathing speeds up for a moment and he starts to cry, big tears running down his drenched face. Then he grows quiet again. I'm left to do everything myself. It takes hours, far longer than I'd imagined. The urine in the bathroom is the worst, taking all the towels we have in the cabin to clean up. I have to run hot water over them in the bathtub, wring them out again and again. Then I have to wipe up the mud we've tracked in. There's a brown path of it leading from the back door to the bathroom. I'm on my knees scrubbing, cleaning. At last I'm as done as I can be and I take the towels and my own clothes and toss them into the washing machine. Naked, I go to Connor and pull off his things. He doesn't resist. He seems hardly aware that I'm there at all. I lead him to the shower, we wash, I towel us both dry. Then I wrap a blanket around him, push him gently over on the sofa, put a pillow under his head.

"Sleep, sweetheart," I say softly. "When the clothes are all done we'll go."

They take nearly two hours to wash and dry. Connor doesn't sleep, his eyes stay open and wide, but neither does he cry anymore. He doesn't do anything but just lay there, staring into space, breathing shallowly, shivering. I bring another blanket for him, tuck it carefully over him, kiss him on the forehead.

"You'll be okay, sweetheart. Try to sleep."

At last the clothes and towels are done. I'm amazed to realize that it's already four o'clock in the morning; dawn will come soon. I know we have to get out of here, far away, to the end of the earth if possible. As I pull the warm things from the dryer I wonder what's happening. Mrs. McCloud would have called Bill hours ago, maybe six hours back, when it became apparent we were late. He would have said he didn't know but not to worry, his wife would have called him if anything had gone wrong. Would Mr. Blue have called? Did he even realize his son wasn't home?

At least I saved Connor from him, I think. Rescued him from that violent drunk of a father. I did that for Connor. Yes.

By now there must have been more calls. Bill is worried by now, I'm sure he is. I wonder if he realizes that his grandfather's pistol isn't in the drawer where it belongs. No, he's had no reason to check it. He's on the phone, or has been, calling the Youth for America number, trying to find out if we got to the conference. But nobody's answering now, not at four a.m. Maybe he's in an uneasy sleep right now, waiting to hear the sound of my car pulling up in the drive and ready to hear the wild story of what delayed us so drastically, why I didn't call. He's kept Gracie calm, I know, told her there's nothing wrong, Mom will be home soon, don't worry. Part of me feels sad about this in an abstracted way but in truth, Bill and Gracie are no longer real to me. Mrs. McCloud, Mr. Blue are mere ghosts. Kylie a faraway memory. Cutts School a dream. All of them gone, vanished, no longer part of reality, if they ever were.

All that exists now is Connor. Connor and Mona, Mona and Connor. I know we have to get away. If they haven't already, the police will start looking, they'll check with the people who ran the conference, they'll find that we duly registered and that participants remember us. Yes, we were definitely there. But afterwards we seem to have vanished. I never stopped anywhere after we left the convention center; there will be no one to identify us as having gone north. I wonder how long it will take Bill to think of the cabin. And yet the cabin is a hundred miles from what our destination had been. No doubt the search will focus on the main roads and side routes leading from the convention center home, at least for a while. The police will put out—what do they call it in the old crime movies?—an APB on us, on the car, with a description and the license plate number. A woman and two children, a boy and a girl. Wild scenarios will ensue. Perhaps we were carjacked, some crazed criminal forcing his way into the vehicle at a traffic light, holding a gun on me and forcing me to drive—where? It might be anywhere in the country. He might do anything, make us stop the car in the middle of nowhere, rape me, rape Kylie, rape Connor, shoot all of us. By mid-morning everyone connected to the school will know, everyone will be trying to stay calm and hope everything has a simple explanation even as they will have their own scenarios of what might have happened. Not one will bear any resemblance to the truth because not one of them knows about Connor, Connor and me.

I fold and put away all the towels and then go to the sofa, whisper, "Honey? We have to go, honey." He seems to have dropped into a light doze but instantly his eyes pop open. He passively allows me to dress him. "We'll get some breakfast a little later, sweetheart," I say, slipping his sweater over him—he didn't bring his big coat—and adjusting it. I gather up my bag and whatever we've left lying around, lead him out to the car. He seems dazed, unable to walk a straight line. I have him lie down in the back and tell him to go to sleep again while I return to the house, make a final check of things, turn off the lights and lock up. I consider going around back and taking a last look at where we left the girl but I covered it well with bushes and branches and cleaned the shovel we used thoroughly. They'll find the makeshift grave eventually, of course, but with any luck even if they think to come to the cabin they'll find no immediately obvious evidence that we've been here, never bother to search behind the building.

In any case, we'll be long gone. I don't know where. I get in the car, start the engine. Connor is silent, curled up horizontally in the back seat. I pull out of the driveway and head down the mountain road, the headlights ghostlike before us. I drive for what seems like a long time on a little paved road until finally I see lighted signs up ahead directing me to go left in order to get to the freeway. I do. I drive a long time again, finally see signs of life, street lights, fast-food restaurants, a sign telling me that the exit for Route 76 is a half-mile ahead. When I get there I take, for no particular reason, the fork that directs us west. The sun is coming up now, behind the car, shining long shadows before us. I drive.

***

In the rear view mirror I can see that Connor's eyes are open, but he doesn't move. He simply lies there curled up in a fetal position. After a while I realize that he's put his thumb into his mouth and he's sucking it.

***

I ask him to sit up as we approach a McDonald's drive-thru, but he doesn't move, doesn't react. I end up pulling to the side of the road, reaching to the seat behind and physically propping him up. I don't have to tell him to stay quiet. He's not spoken in hours. His eyes are glassy. I pull up, order some breakfast sandwiches, get coffee for myself and orange juice for him, pay cash, pull away without incident. I take my own items and place the bag with Connor's food behind me, between the seats.

"Connor? Here's your breakfast. Have something to eat, sweetheart."

I'm suddenly ravenous, virtually inhale the little muffin sandwich I've purchased for myself, slurp down the coffee with no sweetener or cream, scalding my mouth as I do it. I see in the rear view mirror that Connor has made no motion toward the bag, no motion of any kind.

"Honey? Your breakfast. You need to eat something."

As we pull onto the freeway again I wince as I see a state trooper's vehicle move up behind us. I slow, but not too much. I try not to act suspicious. Absurdly it crosses my mind that I could get in trouble for Connor not wearing his seat belt. After a minute or two the trooper pulls into the next lane, passes us.

I find myself growing concerned about the car we're in, the fact that any attentive policeman who pulls up behind us need do no more than read the license number to end everything for us. A movie memory touches my mind and I say, "Hey Connor, remember in *Psycho,* when the lady switches cars? After she's run away with the money, before she gets to the Bates Motel? Do you think we should do that? It might be safer." He doesn't respond. But then it occurs to me that any car dealer today is likely to give me much more trouble about the ownership of the vehicle than California Charlie gave

Marion in *Psycho*. I have my i.d. and the car's registration slip but not the title—that's back home in a file drawer. No, I realize, it will never work. A woman with a virtually comatose young boy in tow trying to sell a car out of state without a title certificate? Anyway, the dealer would no doubt do some sort of routine check on the license number as soon as I said I wanted to sell the car. No. Completely out of the question.

I keep driving, staying to the interstate, speeding but only moderately, staying with most of the traffic. Driving too slow, after all, would be as conspicuous as driving too fast. Hours go by, we pass into Ohio. The traffic signs look slightly different but otherwise it's the same, just a wide ribbon of road endlessly churning under the car.

At last Connor speaks. "Where are we?" he says.

"Hey," I say chirpily, "you're back, huh? With me again? We're in Ohio, sweetheart. We passed a place called Wheeling a while back."

"Where's that?"

"Well, it's in Ohio. Other than that I don't know."

I glance at him in the mirror. He's looking out the side window now, eyes dull, face pale. My hope that he was returning to normal was premature. Connor looks bad, as if all color had been drained from his face by some sort of vampire. The apple glow is long gone, unimaginable on this sallow husk of a child. He doesn't ask why we're in Ohio or where we're going. He just stares uninterestedly out at the passing landscape.

"Where's Kylie?" he says at last.

I frown, look at him.

"She's not with us now, Connor."

After a while he says, "Oh." He doesn't speak again for hours.

***

We stop at another McDonald's for food and a bathroom. Connor doesn't want to get out of the car so I pull at him, force him up gently, encourage him. "C'mon, sweetheart, c'mon, time for a bathroom break."

"I don't want a bathroom break."

"Well, *I* do. C'mon. I want you to go in and use the bathroom."

He's passive about it, allows himself to be supported by my arm. We step into the McDonald's. I'm worried about leaving him alone in the men's room—I wonder if he'll come back out—when I see a Godsend: one of those so-called "family" restrooms. I hustle him into it, lock the door behind us. If anyone wonders why I'm in the bathroom with a boy this age I'll tell them he's a special-needs child—God knows he's acting like one. There's a toilet, a sink, a baby-changing station. He allows me to pull his pants down, aim him at the bowl: "C'mon, sweetheart, time to go pee." He doesn't, he just stands there. After a while his body starts to shake. I try to comfort him but his shaking only seems to grow worse. Finally I arrange his clothes again, then use the toilet myself; Connor stares at me the whole time but doesn't seem to actually *see* me. I wash my hands, open the door for us to step out, lay on supportive mother-talk: "Okay, sweetheart? Feel better now? Are you ready to get some food? Are you hungry? What do you think you want, honey?" He says nothing. I hold him close. His skin is cold. I get us more food, keep up the talk as I move us to the car. This time I put him in the front seat. I buckle his seat belt for him and we pull quickly back out onto the freeway.

We drive, drive for hours. I play the radio for a while but then shut it off. Connor eats nothing, drinks nothing. I can't tell if he's shaking now. Still ravenous, I end up eating his Big Mac for him once it's gone cold and gluey. I watch the road-ribbon unfurl, unfurl. The sun skates across the sky and soon it's growing dark.

Somewhere near the Indiana border I pull off the interstate and drive for a while on some little access road until I come upon a nondescript little town, hardly anything at all. But there's a motel, "Big Ben's." It's like any little motel in the middle of nowhere, interchangeable with dozens of others Connor and I have stayed in, just as the McDonalds' we've been stopping at are interchangeable, as the miles of freeway we've crossed are interchangeable. A large-bellied man is behind the counter—Big Ben, I assume—and I sign us in while Connor waits in the car. "You're in luck," says the man who is probably Big Ben. "I can give you our suite. No extra charge."

I thank him, ask about food, he directs me to some vending machines outside the office, I push in change and pull handles to get us cookies, candy bars, potato chips, sodas. I pull the car around to the side of the building, nearer the room Big Ben has given us, but also farther from the road. I back into the space so that no one from the street can see the car's license plate. I guide Connor into the room. It's like guiding a blind boy. Part of me wants to slip sunglasses over his blank, wide-staring eyes.

The "suite" turns out to be two somewhat rundown rooms with two beds—a queen-sized in the main room and a narrow double in the smaller side room. There's a TV with, as the sign outside proudly proclaims, "Free Cable!" The rooms smell vaguely moldy. But the bathroom is clean enough, and includes a small tub. After I'm done investigating I return to the main room and find Connor sitting on the big bed, unresponsive. I feel his forehead. He's frighteningly cold. It occurs to me that he's in shock, some kind of shock, has been for many hours now. I try to remember my first aid training.

"Connor, honey, lie back, lie back on the bed."

Using pillows I elevate his legs. I check his pulse, which seems normal—shock victims have rapid pulses, I think I remember. Having more or less exhausted what I recall about treating shock, I take a washcloth from the bathroom and soak it with warm water, apply it gently to his forehead.

"Connor, sweetheart, you're going to be all right. Close your eyes. Try to sleep, honey."

I hum to him, no particular tune, just hum, in part to comfort him, in part to keep silence from descending in this room. I reach to his eyelids gently, push them closed as one would a corpse's. After a while I take a cup of water and try to dribble a little into his mouth, wet his lips. He just stays like that, seemingly asleep for all I can tell. But he's not asleep. He's something else, somewhere else. I don't know where he is.

But after a long time his breathing slows and he does seem to have drifted off. I stay very quiet, watching him. His color is bad but his breathing is all right and he's not shaking. It grows dark outside. I go to the window, glance out the curtain. The car is in total darkness, there's no light on this part of the parking lot at all. No one will come for us tonight, I think. Most likely no one is looking within even hundreds of miles of where we are. And yet I know that someone will come, eventually. Someone will knock on some door somewhere or a highway patrolman or policeman or trooper will flash his lights behind us. But is that true? Aren't there stories of people who vanish entirely from their own lives, take on new identities, live somewhere else for years, decades, make new families, new existences? Yes. People do it. I know they do.

After a long time Connor coughs suddenly and I go to him.

"Hey, baby," I whisper in the semi-darkness of the room. "How you feeling?"

"I'm thirsty," he says, not opening his eyes.

I tilt up his head, offer him some water from the cup. He drinks, coughs a little, swallows. Then again, and again. Finally the coughing stops and he's able to drink without trouble. He opens his eyes and looks at me.

"Where are we, Mona?"

"I think we're still in Ohio. But I'm not sure what this town is called. The middle of nowhere."

"When are we going home?"

I think about how to answer this sleepy, sick boy. "Soon, sweetheart."

"Where's Kylie?"

I look at him. "She's not with us on this trip, Connor."

"Oh." He swallows a little more water. "I thought she was." His voice doesn't rise above a whisper.

"No, sweetheart."

He rests his head on the pillow again, bunches the blankets up to his neck. "I'm cold."

He shouldn't be cold; it's actually quite warm in the room. I stroke his forehead again. "I'll run you a hot bath, Connor," I say. He doesn't object, so I get up and do it. When it's ready I return to him. "C'mon, sweetheart. A bath will warm you up." I pull at him gently, get him out of bed, guide him to the bathroom, take off his things for him, help him in. He trembles as I trickle the hot water over his head with a washcloth.

"Good?"

He doesn't say anything. I wash his unresisting limbs and face, watch him soak for a while. His body calms.

"Okay, honey, c'mon," I say at last. "Time to get out." I hold out the biggest towel I can find, ready for him to step into it. He does. I rub him dry, lead him back to the bed, help him get in between the covers.

"Okay?" I ask.

He nods.

I take a quick shower, dry myself, climb into the bed. He's facing away from me. I spoon him, wrap myself around him as tightly and as warmly as I can, try to will some of my strength into his frail body. After a while he begins to shake again.

"Are you cold?" I whisper.

"No."

But he keeps shaking. The shaking becomes violent, frightening, wild thrashings. I hold onto him, feeling that if I let go he might completely fly apart. "Shh, Connor, shh." I hold him, hold him. He begins to cry, first quietly, then wildly, without any reserve, terrible agonized wailings. I hold his forehead, kiss his hair, tell him it's all right, everything will be all right. When he gets too loud I place a pillow gently over his mouth. He screams into it, weeps, hiccoughs. I know I have to stay here, hold him, not let him go, not ever. It suddenly occurs to me that he could die without me, that if I were to get up and leave him now he might literally shake himself apart, cry himself to death.

"Connor," I whisper into his ear, "come back. Come back. Bring yourself back to me. Come on. Come back, Connor."

It goes on for a long time, the weeping, the screaming. But I ask him over and over, hundreds of times, to come back, come back to me. Finally it all slows. Quiets. The shaking fades to occasional tremors. The crying stops. He sucks his thumb.

He whispers something. I don't catch it. I lean to his lips. "What, sweetheart?"

"I want," he whispers hoarsely, "my mom."

"I'm here, sweetheart," I whisper in return. "I'm right here."

***

He sleeps. In the middle of the night he wakes again and says he's thirsty, thirsty and a little hungry. I give him more water, give him half of a giant cookie I bought from the vending machine. I eat the remainder and we get cookie crumbs in the bed. I almost think he smiles, just slightly, a mere shadow of a smile, when I say what a couple of pigs we are and make an oinking sound at him. He rests again, falls asleep again. I do too. Toward morning, my arms still wrapped tightly around his narrow shoulders, my breasts on his back, my legs pushed against his, I see he's gotten an erection. I reach over, stroke it gently. He's asleep, I can tell from his deep breathing. After a few minutes he moans softly and ejaculates into the sheets. He never wakes, not really, just sighs a little. After a while he turns over, his body relaxing into mine, and we sleep that way until the sun's up. Face-to-face. Soul-to-soul.

21

The problem is that I'm running out of money. My own account is nearly depleted and I'm worried every time I make a withdrawal, make sure that we're moving on immediately afterward so that we'll be hundreds of miles away by the time anyone could trace the account activity. I have credit cards but these seem even more dangerous to use. Yet we have to have something. It's amazing how quickly motel rooms, food, gas add up. We drive, drive, Illinois, Missouri, Nebraska, Kansas, the interstates all bleeding into each other, one endless gray-black ribbon of road stretching endlessly before us, endlessly behind us. I have no idea if anyone is following us, if anyone has the slightest idea where we are. I keep us moving, driving all night sometimes, into the following day. We follow no route, just drive, take exits impulsively, get back on the freeway for no reason, change direction, zigzag across counties and states. Connor rarely speaks. He eats when we go to a drive-thru, occasionally he fiddles with the radio, but mostly he just stares out the window. When we get to a motel, invariably out of the way, well off the freeway, he steps into the room and turns on the TV. I always initiate the lovemaking. He never says no, never says yes, just does it with a dispassion I find disturbing but that there's nothing I can do about, at least not now. I understand that he's adjusting to this new life, new reality. I don't want to push him, don't want to frighten him any more than he's already been frightened. I know he'll come around fully, be the apple-cheeked boy I once knew, the sweet bright boy who couldn't wait to be with me under the Christmas tree all those years ago—no, not years, months, it only *feels* like years. I just have to be patient, let him adjust in his own way. I try to josh him along, point out interesting landmarks, stop once in a while if something looks worth stopping for. Yet I'm nervous about letting him be around people. I'm very aware that he could walk up to any one of them, say *My name is Connor Blue, please call the police, I believe they're looking for me* and it would all be over. Yet I can't believe he would really do that, not Connor, not *my* Connor. But he has odd moments, sometimes in the car, sometimes in a room, when his eyes grow strange and he says something disconnected like "Do we have any homework tonight?" or "Where's Kylie?" There's nothing I can do but go along, say, "No, no homework tonight, Connor," or "She's not with us now, Connor." My answers always satisfy him, for that moment. But then the next moment comes. And the next.

Once upon a time in a dream I was Mona Straw and I lived in a lovely middle-class home in Silver Spring Maryland with my husband Bill and daughter Gracie and I taught children at Cutts School and my life was all anyone could ever ask of a life. Billions of people look for food and water and shelter every day on this planet and they go to bed hungry and their children die with their stomachs bulging and flies on their cracked lips and that's when they're not rounded up by armies, by juntas that haul away the boys and force them to carry guns and murder and pillage and line the rest up against a wall and shoot them or hack off their heads except for the pretty daughters, of course, who get raped by a dozen soldiers or two dozen and spat on and beaten and finally wind up with a bullet in the brain or a bayonet in the chest and by that time they welcome it as a blessed relief. That's how people live in this world but it was not how Mona Straw lived once upon a time. In a dream Mona Straw had everything anyone could want or need, far more than she deserved, than anyone really *deserves*. But it wasn't real. Reality is only Connor, Connor Blue, my love, my life. The rest is fantasy. Bill never existed. Gracie never lived. There is no house in Silver Spring Maryland, no Cutts School. There couldn't have been, because there had been no Mona Straw, not *that* Mona Straw, that half-girl, one leg, one arm, half a head. She never existed. Nothing else ever existed except what I see before me right now, the road, the car, the steering wheel in my hands, and Connor, Connor, Connor.

***

One night we lay in bed with Cokes and potato chips and watch *Gun Crazy,* an old '50s film noir. We're both enraptured, Connor leaning toward the screen and shouting "Wow!" every time something new happens. It's just like it was once, only better, now Connor and I don't have to hide behind a veneer of respectability, appropriateness, we can do what we wanted to do then, be naked together, crawl into bed, touch each other, fill the bed with crumbs if we want to, and just escape into movieland, watch, watch, then make love afterward, make love all night long. I've not seen Connor like this in a long time. I've never been more joyful, more ecstatic, life is everything I want it to be, I have everything I'll ever need in this room, this bed. We laugh, we wrestle with each other during the commercials, we play silly games with fingers and toes, we kiss, then the movie pulls us back, again and again, always the movie, the movie on the screen, the movie of our life. It occurs to me that I don't know what town we're in or even what state. It makes no difference. My state is Connor Blue. My life is Connor Blue. This night, I think, he's finally better, he's committed to me again, to us, his life is my life. He laughs, the color comes back to his cheeks, he's a boy again, a happy boy with his first love.

***

It doesn't last. That night in the middle of the night I awaken to the sound of his crying and when I touch him he pulls away, yanks his shoulder from under my touch. I don't ask him why he's crying. I don't say anything. I can't think of anything to say. After a while he says, "I want to go back to school." Later still he says, "I wish Kylie was here." After that he says, "Mona? I want to go home, Mona."

***

And so I watch him, watch him carefully. I don't allow him in public places without me. He doesn't resist, doesn't fight. Many times he's quite affectionate, holding my hand as we wait for our fast food to arrive or wandering around a park or on a street somewhere. He laughs, he swings our hands high together, he runs ahead and says, "Catch me!" At night we can still love, be in love, watch old movies on whatever local station the TV picks up. One night it's *You Only Live Once,* another it's *They Live By Night,* wonderful dark stories, lovers on the lam. He's Connor then, the old Connor, the Connor I love, will love until death.

***

But somewhere outside Oklahoma City in a dry dusty town, not even a town, just a scattershot collection of rundown buildings of which the biggest is the *Tumbleweed Motel,* where we stay, it happens, the moment I've feared. In the dark after TV and a vending machine dinner and lovemaking for hours I nod off to sleep and when I wake he's not there. Connor is not there. The bed is empty, the bathroom is empty. I slip on my shirt and jeans and look outside, walk over to the ice machines, look toward the office (dark now, closed). Nothing. Nothing, nothing! I try to breathe, try to think. *He's gone. He's gone.* But he can't have gone far, on foot. And what's around here? Nothing. The town is lightless, everyone asleep. There are hardly any streetlamps. Only one road in and out. He couldn't have knocked on anybody's door, I'd see the light from here, there would be cars and police lights bearing down on this motel. I can't call out, can't let the owners know I've lost my *son,* can't wake the occupants of the other rooms—there are two or three, judging from the cars in the lot. I collect my keys, get in the car, gather up my bag which I always leave in the locked vehicle when we take a room. He can only have gone

one of two ways. I take a left, headlights sweeping over all that endless Oklahoma dirt, drive for four miles. I've gone the wrong way. He couldn't have gotten this far. Unless, of course, he didn't stay on the road at all, instead wandered off into the desert. But that would be crazy. He *must* be on the road. I turn around, gun the engine and drive as fast as I dare to in order to make up the four miles I've wasted. At last I'm back at the motel. I pass it by, slow down and keep driving, driving. He's about two miles from the motel. When he sees the lights he turns around and begins to wave but then realizes that it's me. He runs then, runs into the dirt, past all the thorny brush. I pull up, take the gun from my bag. I don't point it at him. I just stand there in the glare of the headlights.

"Connor, come back here."

He squints in the light that's aimed straight at him. He looks at me.

"I don't want to, Mona."

"Yes, you do. Come back, sweetheart. Come back to me."

He stands indecisively, looks over his shoulder at the desert dark.

"There's nothing out there, Connor," I say. "Nothing but dirt and tumbleweed and rattlesnakes." I smile. He can't see it but I'm sure he hears it in my voice. "Back at the motel you can watch TV all night long if you want. And you can make love to me all night long if you want."

"Mona…"

"Come back to me, sweetheart. Now."

Finally he steps slowly toward me, gets obligingly in the car. I get in as well, return the gun to its bag, turn the car around and return to the motel. When we get to the room and close the door behind us I hug him gently and say, "I meant what I said, Connor. Do you want to watch TV all night? Or make love? Or both?"

"I just want to go to sleep," he says, not looking at me. He removes his shirt and pants, climbs into the bed wearing only his shorts. I follow him, take off my things, get in with him, stroke his warm shoulders.

After a minute he says, quietly: "Please don't touch me."

I withdraw my hands. I watch him in the darkness.

***

Another county, another state. I've nearly maxed my credit cards. I know I should be thinking of how we can have a life together, really *live* as opposed to this fugitive quasi-existence. Back at the beginning with Connor I'd hated the furtive quality of our encounters, hated having to rent dirty motel rooms when what I really wanted to do was announce our love to everyone, to have Connor make love to me on the street, the lawn, in front of my classes, boldly, shamelessly. Back in that other life, that fantasy life, that dream. But the furtiveness never stopped and it hasn't stopped now, we're still running, still hiding. But I can't trust him anymore. I keep the bag with the pistol with me all the time now. I see his wandering eyes when we're in public places. I notice how he looks around, maybe checking where he could run if he decided to. I see. It will end, whether they are close upon us or not. It will end. Connor's going to end it. I know it.

But I can't let him.

22

Connor's green eyes watch me. He's handcuffed to the bed, arms raised above him. I've used one of his white T-shirts to make a gag I've tied around his mouth. We've been like this for nearly two days. When I checked into this motel by the sea I paid for several days in advance, asked that we not be bothered, placed the *Do Not Disturb* sign on the outside doorknob. We haven't been disturbed. The maid leaves towels outside the room.

I don't know where we are except that we've arrived at the ocean. Oregon? California? Everything blurs. I can hear the sea close by when I turn down the volume on the TV, but mostly I leave it up so that Connor can watch. I try to keep him as comfortable as I can. I know the handcuffs must be awkward. I locked his wrists into them when he was asleep, locked the cuffs onto the heavy metal bedposts. He woke as I wrapped the gag around him. He tried to scream, shook the bed violently, again and again, for hours. "Sweetheart," I kept telling him, "this will really be easier if you just calm down." I brought the gun from my bag, held it at my side. "It's not like you can get away. You don't want to anyway, do you? I know you don't. I know you love me. I know you're just scared now, that's all. Shh. Settle down, Connor. Quiet down." I don't like it but it was the only way. I could see in his eyes that he was going to run, he was going to leave me.

It does create practical problems. There's no way for Connor to go to the bathroom. I tried to use a towel, to put it under him, and it worked somewhat but not really. Now there are yellow streams on his shorts, which is all he's wearing. There are yellow streaks all over the bed. I still sleep with him, I don't mind. But I'm afraid he hasn't eaten anything in a long time, or had anything to drink. He'll start screaming if I loosen the gag, I know. My only option is to let him weaken to the point that he can't scream, then I'll take off the gag and feed him, give him water, nurse him back to health and strength and by doing that he'll realize again how much I love him, how I'll never stop loving him.

We've been in this room forever, but we're not in this room at all. Nothing is real now. I wander around as in a dream, as if I were in a film, both of us. The other life wasn't my life, but this room with Connor is just as fantastical now. Once upon a time we were in love, once upon a time Connor didn't think it *dirty* and it wasn't. Once upon a time it was the two of us against the world and it can be again, I know it can, if only I can prove to him my love.

In my endless pacing in the room I occasionally get a glimpse of myself in the bathroom mirror and this reinforces the idea that this isn't my life, this isn't me. The person looking back at me is clearly mad, her hair every which way, her eyes skittish and wild, black pockets under them. Her expression is somehow different than the old Mona Straw, from that other unreal life, somehow lopsided, unbalanced. *Feral.* Her movements are sudden, graceless, erratic. Her skin is greasy. Her clothes are soiled. Who is it that can tell me who I am?

Day collides with night and then suddenly it's day again. Once or twice someone knocks on the door and I tell them thank you, we're sleeping, just leave the towels and sheets outside the door. They do. We're paid up, after all, we're not bothering anyone. The *Sea Breeze Inn,* that's the name of this place. Ocean outside but no beach, nothing but rocks and gray skies. Salt air. A four-lane road a short distance down the hill, surprisingly busy day and night. The traffic makes me feel nervous, vulnerable, but there's no changing now. No going back.

I used to have fantasies about a life I'd lived. I was a teacher, a wife, a mother. I remember names: Bill. Gracie. Cutts. All those children. None of them existed, I'm sure. They were a dream I had. But this doesn't exist either, this room, this boy in the pink handcuffs on the urine-stained bed. How could it? This can't be my life.

It's night again.

"I'm not dirty, Connor," I say, my voice strange in my throat, hoarse, husky. "We're not dirty. Nothing we did was dirty."

To prove it to him I slip the pistol into my belt, sit next to him on the bed. I take one of his feet. Initially he resists but then I say, "Relax, sweetheart, I'm not going to hurt you, Mona would never hurt you," and I look at it. He had been walking barefoot outside not long before he came in to sleep and there are bits of grass between his toes, even some dark substance, oil or grease. I go to the bathroom, wet a towel, bring it to the bed.

"Sweetheart? Let me wash your feet. They're not clean. Come on. Don't be shy. You're dirty."

I hold his foot carefully, nuzzle it with my cheek, wash it with the cloth. Then I pick up the other. Yet he still looks suspicious, frightened.

"Clean," I whisper. "Clean, clean, clean, clean, clean."

Then I begin licking his foot. I will lick his foot clean, his entire body, and when he is completely clean he'll see that all I ever offered him was clean. I consider biting down on his foot, tearing it in half, eating it, eating him, making us part of each other forever, but no. That wouldn't be right. It wouldn't be clean.

I suddenly realize that there are red and blue lights flashing outside the window. I jump up, my breath shallow. I hear footsteps, boots on the gravel outside. I take the gun in my hands. I lean close to Connor, sidle up next to him. I let him see me switch off the safety. I let him watch me cock it. I feel light, even blissful. None of this is happening, not to me. This is not my life.

I hold the barrel close to his eye so he can peer down into its darkness. He's shaking his head, quivering, trying to scream through the gag.

Then I move the barrel to my own temple.

I hold eye contact with him as I slowly squeeze the trigger.

Snap.

His eyes widen and I hear myself laughing. I've never laughed like this. It's a high-pitched sound, very different from my usual laugh. As I laugh, or someone who looks like me does, there's a knock at the door. It's a strong, masculine knock.

"Police. Open the door, please."

My laughter settles for a moment. I point the gun straight at Connor, cock it again and again. *Snap, snap, snap, snap, snap.*

"The movie's over now, sweetheart," I say, or someone does. "I'm sorry it didn't have a better ending."

I stand then. The knock comes again, louder this time. I hear my laughter reverberating throughout the room, echoing off the walls, bouncing through my brain, laughter that once started can never stop, will never stop until the end of the world, the end of time. Gun in hand, laughing, shrieking, screaming, I move to the door. I unlock it.

I pull it open.

Epilogue

Some of what I've written here is true.

But in fact, there are great swaths I don't remember, and even more I never knew. I was only eleven, after all.

I've tried to portray Mona as I remember her. It's difficult, nearly fifteen years later. Much of what happened between us has remained unvisited territory in my memory, dark and unwanted, and so I've lost a lot of it over the years.

The facts are accurate, to the best of my knowledge. Some of them come not from my own remembrance but from news articles of the time as well as a book or two that was written about the case. A few bits and pieces I learned from her husband Bill not long before he moved with Gracie away from the Silver Spring area and vanished from my life.

What I don't know, of course, what I've imagined here, is what it was like to *be* Mona Straw. Her thoughts, her perceptions. And yet that seemed the only way to record this, the only way to make it *worth* recording. To, in a sense, become her. To try to understand what perhaps defies understanding.

Is what I've written fiction, then? I don't think so. It's truth, but of a different sort.

They made a movie about the case—they called it *Savaging the Dark*. Maybe you saw it. I had nothing to do with the film, other than getting a fee for it. It was quite a large fee. My father managed to spend a lot of it in the couple of years before he died, but enough was left that it put me through college. And they changed the names, so I didn't have to cringe every time I told people my name was *Connor Blue*. Since I was a minor at the time my name rarely appeared in news reports about the case anyway, but it did leak out here and there on the Internet, which was a new thing then. Still, for most people "Mona Straw's eleven-year-old kidnapping victim" was utterly anonymous. Nameless. Faceless.

It was a pretty good movie. I saw it one afternoon by myself, just walked into a theater in the town where I was going to college, paid my admission and watched it. How accurate was it? Not very. But there were a few scenes, especially the early ones, when the Mona character—they called her "Mindy"—is getting to know the boy, "Colin," that rang true, that touched soft bells of memory. Occasionally when I'm channel surfing I come across the film on cable even now, watch a few minutes of it. Generally it doesn't seem to have anything to do with me at all. I think Mona would have liked it, actually. It's not *High Sierra* or *Strangers on a Train,* but it's not bad. Roger Ebert gave it three stars.

I've been back to Silver Spring a few times in the years since, sometimes alone, sometimes with my wife. I always visit Kylie McCloud's grave, always place flowers before the headstone, and her mother's next to it. But I don't cry. It was simply too long ago and I just remember too little. The Kylie I've described here, in my Mona-narrative, is mostly fiction.

She was small, she read a lot, she wore glasses that slipped down her nose. Beyond that it's mostly a darkness to me. But I wonder. When I make up the details, are they just my imagination? Or are they actual memories returning to me, tugging at my mind's sleeve?

I don't know.

What I do know is that the movie got the end of the story completely wrong. Mona did not die in that violent shootout you saw on screen. Her end was much stranger than that. It turned out that the police weren't even there for us; they had no idea who we were. Instead there had been an armed robbery nearby and the police were simply canvassing the area to see if there were any witnesses. That's it. It had nothing to do with us. When she opened the door the policeman began to ask his routine questions but Mona's hysterical laughter stopped him. Then he saw the gun in her hand, back-stepped fast, started to draw his own weapon. Mona ran. At some point she dropped the gun. Shrieking, screaming, she charged through the parking lot and out onto the busy road facing the motel. An SUV crashed into her.

A silver key ring was found in the road, knocked from her pocket. It held a key to the handcuffs, and they used it to free me.

I was in the hospital then, for a very long time. Several hospitals, actually.

But in the end I came out and resumed my life. I went to a different school, a smaller one, a kind of therapeutic place. I liked it. I attended a regular high school and did as well as most. I met Linda—my wife, eventually—in college. Our first child, a daughter, is on the way.

What do I do for a living? Oddly enough, I'm a CPA. That same math that was such a darkness to me in middle school opened up to me later, became strangely comforting and beautiful to me, maybe because it represented a world over which I could exert total control. I don't know. It's as good a theory as any. I'm happy enough in my job, anyway.

I mentioned that I've revisited the Silver Spring area from time to time and stopped by Kylie McCloud's grave. Until recently I'd never visited Mona's, which is in a different cemetery, in Washington itself. Finally I did, not very long ago. It was a perfectly clear spring day, a light breeze, very comfortable. I happened to find her parents' stones first; then, next to them, her brother Michael's. Finally hers. I stepped up to it, one of those simple gray plaques they embed in the lawn. It said *Mona Straw* along with her dates. That was all.

I stood there in the lengthening shadows of an April afternoon looking down at the name, shifting the flowers I'd brought along from hand to hand. When I bought them I wasn't sure I would leave them for her. Perhaps, I thought, I'd just place them on a random stranger's grave and go. But as I stood there it felt right, somehow, to set them there, so I did. Half-a-dozen white roses. Nothing too fancy.

I knew I would never come to her grave again.

And yet I also knew that, in her way, Mona had loved me. Perhaps part of her—the sick, confused part—was really loving someone else, someone she lost, someone I resembled and whose sudden death had broken her, broken her for all time, even if she didn't know it. But there was another part of her that truly loved me, loved me more than anyone should ever love another person.

Again, I don't know.

But I cried for her then, the only time I've ever cried for her or ever will. And I cried for Kylie McCloud and her mother and Bill and Gracie and for all the loss, the damage, the irretrievable black years of my own life.

When I was finished I knelt down and touched the flowers, ran my fingers across the engraved shapes of the letters of her name. Then I walked back to the parking lot, got into my car, and drove away.

About the Author

Christopher Conlon is best known as the editor of the Bram Stoker Award-winning Richard Matheson tribute anthology *He Is Legend*, which was a selection of the Science Fiction Book Club and which has appeared in multiple foreign translations. He is the author of several novels, including the Stoker Award finalists *Midnight on Mourn Street* and *A Matrix of Angels*, as well as five volumes of short stories, four books of poetry, and a play. A former Peace Corps volunteer, Conlon holds an M.A. in American Literature from the University of Maryland. He lives in the Washington, D.C. area. Visit him online at http://christopherconlon.com.